JACKRABBIT JINGLE BELLS

The Morgan sisters are back ... just in time for Christmas!

Ronnie groaned, slumping down in the seat as Kate yanked open the driver's side door.

"I told you to stop calling me 'crazy'!" the Pregosaurus Rex screamed and slung her purse at Claire.

The leather bag hit her in the shoulder—hard—before tumbling to the floor at her feet. "Ouch!" She glared at Kate, who was settling in behind the steering wheel. "What the hell do you have in there?" She reached down and picked up the purse. "A frickin' boulder?"

Ronnie snickered. "It's an over the shoulder boulder holder." When Kate frowned at Jackie-Junior in the rearview mirror, Ronnie added, "You know, what Chester calls 'bras.' Only in this case, it really is an actual over the shoulder bould—"

"We get it, Cousin Eddie," Claire cut her off.

"Who's Cousin Eddie?" Ronnie asked.

Kate turned in her seat. "The dorky guy from *National Lampoon's Christmas Vacation.*"

"Oh, yeah." Ronnie slapped Claire's shoulder. "I'm not a dork."

"I never said you were, your little sister did." Claire started to unzip Kate's purse to check out what was inside. The knocked-up nutter wasn't packing heat again, was she?

Also by Ann Charles

JACKRABBIT JINGLE BALLS

A JACKRABBIT JUNCTION NOVELLA

Book 4.7

Ann Charles

Illustrations by C.S. Kunkle

For all of those who have weathered a divorce.

Cover Art by C.S. Kunkle
Cover Design by B Biddles
Editing by Elizabeth M.S. Flynn
Formatting by B Biddles

Library of Congress: 2021921494
E-book ISBN-:13: 978-1-940364-82-7
Print ISBN-:13978-1-940364-81-0

Dear Reader,

The Morgan sisters tales are always a lot of fun to write. Their brand of "trouble" is rough and rowdy, and many days their family dynamics are wonderfully nutty. JACKRABBIT JINGLE BALLS** stays true to the Morgan sisters' brand, but with a dash of divorce turmoil thrown into the pot.

My parents divorced when I was three years old. It wasn't a harmonious split. The aftershocks rumbled for years, shaking both my parents and us kids. As I cruised into adulthood, I was determined not to follow in my parents' path. I would marry for life … or not marry at all.

I was naïve. Or maybe I was just too optimistic. Either way, I got married at the young age of twenty. We tried our best for seven years, but marriage is not for sissies. Thankfully, we had no children, which was a conscious decision on our part. I could feel that marriage crumbling around the edges long before it collapsed, but I was determined to keep trying to fix it—until I gave up. My divorce went much more smoothly than my parents' had, but it was still traumatic and sad and exhausting.

Through both of my firsthand experiences with divorce, family and friends, along with loads of laughter, was the salve that helped to heal the wounds. So, when it came time to tackle this subject in storyland, I knew the Morgan sisters would give it the gritty twist of humor and family drama needed to talk about divorce and the scars it leaves when the dust clears, even if it is holiday time.

I hope you enjoy this story of life, love, divorce, and Christmas!

Ann Charles
www.anncharles.com

**Warning—Don't look up "jingle balls" on the internet. Ha ha ·ha!

Acknowledgments

Very few authors make it to The End, let alone through the publishing gauntlet, on their own. They have spouses who support them, friends who cheer them on, fellow writers who help brainstorm and find plot holes, editors who find those dang grammatical errors, first-draft readers who give helpful feedback, and beta readers who look for those final little buggers that make it through all of the other eyeballs.

I am not one of those "very few authors." I am fortunate to have a lot of people helping me along the way.

Many thanks to the following wonderful helpers for your time, generosity, and kindness:

Sam Lucky and our kids, Beaker and Chicken Noodle.

Jacquie Rogers, Kristy McCaffrey, Diane Garland, Michelle Davison, Amber Holt

Mary Ida Kunkle, Marcia Britton, Margo Taylor, Paul Franklin, Lucinda Nelson, Stephanie Kunkle, Wendy Gildersleeve, Vickie Huskey

Elizabeth M.S. Flynn, Editor

C.S. Kunkle, Illustrator and Cover Artist

Mary Avery, Laura Wollam, Jo Ann Reinhold, Heather Chargualaf, Elaina Boudreaux, Jan Dobbins, Dave Smithwick, Bob Dickerson, Elizabeth Lavasile, Debbie Hawrylyshyn, Brandy Lanfair-Jones, Becky Humphreys, Craig Scott, Melissa Hogan, Rob Grayson.

Cast

Claire Alice Morgan (1,2,3,4,4.5, 4.7)—Main heroine of the series, Mac's girlfriend, Harley's granddaughter

Kathryn "Kate" Morgan (2,3,4,4.5, 4.7)—Claire's younger sister, Deborah's youngest daughter, Butch's girlfriend

Veronica "Ronnie" Morgan (3,4,4.5, 4.7)—Claire's oldest sister, Deborah's oldest daughter, Grady's girlfriend

MacDonald "Mac" Garner (1,2,3,4,4.5,4.7)—Main hero of the series, Claire's boyfriend

Valentine "Butch" Carter (1,2,3,4,4.5,4.7)—Owner of The Shaft, the only bar in Jackrabbit Junction, Kate's boyfriend

Grady Harrison (1,2,3,4,4.5,4.7)—Sheriff of Cholla County, Ronnie's boyfriend

Chester Thomas (1,2,3,4,4.5,4.7)—Harley's old Army vet buddy

Harley "Gramps" Ford (1,2,3,4,4.5,4.7)—Claire's maternal grandfather, Ruby's husband

Ruby Ford (aka Ruby Wayne-Martino) (1,2,3,4,4.5,4.7)—Mac's aunt, owner of the RV park, Harley's wife

Jessica Wayne (1,2,3,4,4.5,4.7)—Ruby's teenage daughter, Harley's stepdaughter

Manuel "Manny" Carrera (1,2,3,4,4.5,4.7)—Harley's old Army vet buddy, Deborah's husband

Deborah Ford-Carrera (2,3,4,4.5,4.7)—Claire's mom, Harley's daughter, Manny's wife

Henry Ford (1,2,3,4,4.7)—Harley's beagle/dog

Randy Morgan (4.7)—The Morgan sisters' dad

Joe Martino (1,2,3,4,4.5,4.7)—Deceased; Ruby's first husband, previous owner of the RV park

Aunt Millie (3,4,4.5,4.7)—Sheriff Harrison's aunt, leader of the library gang

Gary (2,3,4,4.7)—Bartender at The Shaft

Divorce isn't such a tragedy. A tragedy's staying in an unhappy marriage, teaching your children the wrong things about love. Nobody ever died of divorce."

**~Jennifer Weiner
Author**

Chapter One:
Babes in ~~Toyland~~
Jackrabbit-Land

Saturday Night, December 22nd
Yuccaville, Arizona

O nce upon a time, there was a rusty old railroad whistle-stop in a prickly, wind-scoured desert that Santa Claus had left behind for the buzzards to peck the hell out of," Claire Morgan said, starting her Christmas tale.

She had to speak loud enough to be heard over the heavy bass beat throbbing from the overhead speakers in the strip club. Up on the U-shaped stage, several nearly naked babes shook their moneymakers, along with their jingle ball pasties, as they wrapped themselves around candy cane–striped poles much to the delight of the swarm of male, Santa suit–wearing admirers ... along with a few females decked out in Mrs.

Claus costumes, too.

Judging from the boisterous crowd of merry makers, Dirty Gerties' marketing idea for a nudie bar version of the North Pole was a rousing success. If only the ventilation system could keep up with the locker-room smells of stinky armpits, nose-burning cologne, and some cringe-inducing variant of *eau de sex*.

Ding-dong merrily on high! This was not how Claire wanted to spend her Saturday night. First, there were too many people in the place sharing in the festive nakedness. Second, while it was true that Claire had a bit of a colorful history involving bare-assed shenanigans, she suspected that watching Sparkles McSugarbritches blast a crowd of leering Santa Clauses with a large, phallic-looking glitter gun would scar her for many, many Christmases to come.

"That's just silly," Ronnie Morgan said from where she sat slouched next to Claire in the horseshoe-shaped booth, trying to hide behind a double-sided drink menu. Her brown eyes and hair looked black under the seizure-inducing strobe lights.

"What's silly? That hat?" Claire pointed at the limp, felt Santa hat strapped onto her older sister's head. "Just because the bouncer handed you that on the way in the door doesn't mean you have to wear it, you know."

Claire's hat was tucked away in her coat pocket, along with the chocolate mints that had been stuffed inside the door gift. She had a feeling she might need the chocolate later to sweeten up the memory of tonight.

"No, your story is silly. Why would *Santa* leave this place behind?" Ronnie asked. "I mean, unless he has a good reason, like maybe there were gun-toting hitmen lurking in the shadows, waiting to take potshots at him."

Claire scowled at her sister. Ronnie was sort of on the lam thanks to her ex-husband's money-laundering history that had landed him in prison. Only she wasn't running from the law—well, not on most days. Although she did periodically like to give the FBI agents hounding her the runaround. Ronnie was, however, trying to hide from some very, very bad guys that her ex had thrown under the bus in order to lighten his sentence.

"Because Santa wanted to leave this particular town behind, plain and simple," Claire told her. "Don't make this tale too complicated. It's not your crap-tabulous life we're talking about."

Ronnie glared back. "Wow. I'm drowning in your sisterly affection right now."

And that brought Claire to her *third* reason for not wanting to be at Dirty Gerties tonight—her tablemates for the evening shared a significant amount of DNA with her. Whoever said that family bonding improved mental health probably hadn't been forced to sit next to their siblings while their seats bounced due to a five-minute, grunt-filled, ring-ting-tingling "sleigh ride" happening in the booth next door.

As far as Claire was concerned, lap dancers should never be allowed to wear reindeer antlers and glowing Rudolph noses, especially if a grisly-faced Santa wannabe who had shoehorned himself into a red velvet suit was on the Naughty list.

Claire scrubbed both hands down her face. Christmas would never be the same for her again.

Ronnie peeked over the top of the laminated menu, scanning the club for the umpteenth time. "It makes more sense if the protagonist is Father Time," she told Claire, her gaze darting here and there. "Especially with the buzzards involved."

With a growl, Claire snatched the menu from her sister's hands. "It's my Christmas story, you paranoid putz. I'll tell it the way I want to."

"What do you have against Yuccaville, anyway?" Ronnie asked, making a grab for the menu, but Claire held it out of reach. "It's a nice town. A little dusty in the corners, maybe, but the people are friendly."

Not all of them. "You're biased."

"Am not."

"Ever since you started shagging the Cholla County sheriff on a regular basis—"

"Sex has nothing to do with my new positive attitude."

"That's a big bowl of figgy pudding. And don't even try to tell me your Polly Positive pretense is due to that new 'energizing' yoga routine you've been yapping about. We all know those butt-lifting, stretchy pants you like to wear these days are an excuse to go commando."

Her sister's jaw dropped. "You're wrong. I wear them because they're comfortable and they're good for my circulation."

Laughing, Claire said, "Please. Lighting up Sheriff Harrison's Christmas tree is what they're really good for."

"You really need to stop ending your sentences with prepositions, Claire." Kate Morgan horned into their conversation from her place on the other side of Ronnie.

Claire rolled her eyes. "Nobody asked you to share your English expertise, Pregosaurus Rex."

Holding down the heel of the horseshoe booth, Claire's younger sister was situated so she could make a quick escape to the bathroom, if needed. Coming up on four months into her first pregnancy, Kate spent a portion of her day with her pretty blond head parked over the commode, reading any floating bits of toilet paper like they were tea leaves. Although, thankfully, her bouts of nausea seemed to be calming down as of late. Unfortunately, the mad monkey in her head was still throwing bananas at anyone who dared to venture too close to her cage.

"With all of the college classes you have under your belt," Kate continued, "your vernacular shortcomings are truly sad."

Even though Kate had officially quit teaching last summer, she couldn't muffle the grammar cop patrolling her airwaves.

"Stuff a stocking in it, Einstein." Claire mimed zipping her lips. "Or I'll tell your baby daddy that you're planning to weasel out of meeting his parents this Christmas."

Kate's eyes widened. "You wouldn't dare!"

Claire shrugged. "I might."

A commotion down near the far end of the stage caught her attention. One of Santa's buxom elves appeared to be using her very large sugarplums to polish a candy cane pole while her admirers hooted and hollered. Claire grimaced. That poor elf was going to end up with a hell of a set of blisters if she didn't change up her routine soon.

Kate leaned over the table, blocking Claire's view. "You pinkie promised."

Oh, yeah. "But my legs were crossed at the time."

Ronnie snorted loud enough to be heard above the hip-grinding music. "That's a first for you, Miss Butter Thighs. Your lover boy must not have been within a five-mile radius."

" 'Butter thighs'?" Claire poked Ronnie in the ribs, making her squirm.

Kate grinned. "When is Mac coming back, anyway?"

Claire's so-called lover boy had been working long hours for the last few weeks at a jobsite south of Tucson so that he could stay in Jackrabbit Junction over the Christmas holiday. Claire had opted to remain at the Dancing Winnebagos RV Park with her family over the last month, spending her days working at the campground rather than hanging out all alone in Mac's house in the city.

"Tomorrow morning sometime," Claire told her. "He's going to try to be here before Dad shows up."

"Why?" Ronnie smirked. "So he can watch Mom's head explode when Dad's girlfriend steps out of the car?"

Claire groaned. As much as she loved her father, his insistence on spending the holiday down here in Arizona with them made her gut churn. Or maybe it was the tube of sugar cookie dough she'd bought at the store this morning and scarfed in one sitting.

Speaking of their mother, Deborah Ford-Carrera was heading her way across the strip club, fresh from the ladies' room where she'd gone to "powder her nose" and apparently poof up her mid-length blond hair so that it framed her head like a feathery bonnet. Her pink *New Bride* sash glowed brightly against the backdrop of her black party dress each time the stage lights flashed ultraviolet. The half-full drink in her hand sloshed as she stumbled slightly before stopping to glare back at a skinny Santa whose black boots had been in her path.

"Where'd Mom get the drink?" Claire asked.

Ronnie looked in Deborah's direction. "She must have stopped at the bar."

"Please tell me she's not drunk already." Claire frowned. "We've only been here twenty minutes." Hell, they were still waiting for the waitress to come and take their drink orders.

"More like thirty minutes, and I wouldn't put it past Mom to have snuck in her own flask and glass," Kate said. "Her private drinking party runs 24/7 these days."

Yeah, and that was an ongoing problem all three of them were going to have to deal with soon whether they wanted to or not.

"At least she's a happy drunk," Claire said, trying to find something positive about their situation. Ronnie-Polly-Positive must be rubbing off on her.

Ronnie scoffed. "Yeah, when she's not crying in her cognac about her lost youth."

An older version of Kate with a lot sharper teeth, Deborah liked to bemoan how she had wasted the last three-plus decades of her life trying to help her daughters achieve

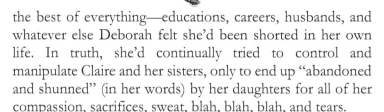

the best of everything—educations, careers, husbands, and whatever else Deborah felt she'd been shorted in her own life. In truth, she'd continually tried to control and manipulate Claire and her sisters, only to end up "abandoned and shunned" (in her words) by her daughters for all of her compassion, sacrifices, sweat, blah, blah, blah, and tears.

And then came the divorce from their father this last summer, which finally put to death a thirty-five-year marriage that had been high on hysterics and low on love.

Over the years, Claire had been amazed at her dad's heroic fortitude when it came to Deborah and their marriage, but she'd never expected him to seek solace in the arms of another woman—and neither had her mom, according to Deborah's many, many tales of woe.

But he had, and very soon, for the first time since having her blinders removed and learning her father was just as human as everyone else, Claire was going to see her hero without his mask and cape. Would she be able to look him in the eyes knowing what he'd done? While she could understand him divorcing her mom, his infidelity sort of grinded on her. They'd talked on the phone a few times since she'd moved to Jackrabbit Junction, but distance had kept everything from feeling too real.

Claire watched their mother, who was now cheering for the gyrating, scantily dressed elf on the stage.

And then there was Dad's girlfriend to consider. She was older than him by a few years, according to her mom. Was she going to end up as their new stepmom soon? How would that work out? It certainly had its pitfalls for Cinderella and Snow White.

Deborah set her glass of liquor down on a nearby table and leaned over the stage near one of the dancer's spiky-heeled boots.

"Did Mom just tip that stripper?" Ronnie asked.

Grimacing, Claire nodded. "Using her teeth, no less."

"Be nice, you two," Kate chastised. "This is Mom's bridal shower, remember? She's here to have fun."

"Belated bridal shower," Ronnie corrected, directing their attention to a bouncer wrestling with a drunken Santa down by another topless elf dancer and her candy cane stripper pole.

Good ol' St. Nick had crawled partway onto the stage, managing to lose his red velvet pants somewhere in the process. The tussle played out under the flashing lights, burning snapshots of bared butt cheeks—and more—into Claire's memory, until the dancer planted her foot on the side of Santa's bare ass and shoved him back into the crowd.

"A strip club bridal shower to boot," Claire said and then sighed. Holy holly berries. She was going to need a full frontal lobotomy after tonight.

"I mean it, you two," Kate continued. "Dad showing up tomorrow is really messing with Mom's head. She hasn't seen him since they parted at the courthouse after their divorce was final last summer."

Ronnie winced, turning to Claire. "This Christmas is going to turn into a shitshow, isn't it?"

"Undoubtedly." Claire turned to their younger sister. "It's too bad you can't drink your way through it like the rest of us." Where was their waitress anyway? Maybe they needed to get their drinks at the bar.

Kate lifted her chin. "I don't need alcohol. I have impending motherhood to keep my spirits lifted."

Claire guffawed. "Who are you and what have you done with Crazy Kate?"

"I told you the other day," Kate said between gritted teeth. "I don't like that nickname."

"How about 'Cuckoo Kate'?" Ronnie offered, chuckling.

Kate held her fist in front of Ronnie's nose. "How about I rearrange your face, Commando?"

"Now girls," their mother said as she slid into the booth

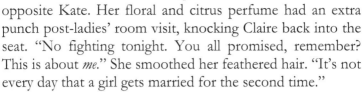

opposite Kate. Her floral and citrus perfume had an extra punch post-ladies' room visit, knocking Claire back into the seat. "No fighting tonight. You all promised, remember? This is about *me*." She smoothed her feathered hair. "It's not every day that a girl gets married for the second time."

As Claire stifled a snort, a red-haired elf approached them wearing Christmas tree nipple pasties topped with jingling dingle balls and a pair of extremely short-shorts. Upon closer inspection, Claire wasn't even sure they qualified as shorts. More like a few strips of stretchy material tied together by tinsel and secured with a candy cane belt.

"Hey gals, I hear we're celebrating a big day over here."

Deborah tittered and leaned toward the waitress. "I eloped to Las Vegas a month ago, so I didn't get to have a bridal shower … until tonight!" She squealed the last part, overplaying her role as a happy bride and edging more toward a fanatical, man-eating bridezilla.

"Well, we'll need to make sure we celebrate the hell out of your weddin' bliss, hon." The waitress pulled an order pad out from somewhere behind her.

Kate leaned to the side, peering around the waitress' mostly bare butt cheek. "Where did you have that thing tucked away?"

"Never mind, Katie," Ronnie said, tugging her sister back upright.

The waitress dislodged a pen from under her elf hat. "What can I get ya girls?"

Ronnie beat Claire to the punch. "I'll have a gin and—"

"Cognacs," Deborah interrupted. "On the rocks. All around." She made a pouty face at her youngest. "Except for Kathryn. She'll take a Shirley Temple."

"I don't drink cognac," Claire told her mom. To the waitress, she said, "A beer will be fine. Something local without too much hops."

"No." Her mother's chin jutted. "It's my party and you're

drinking cognac with me." She smiled at the waitress, all honey without a hint of her usual acid to be heard when she added, "Just bring us a whole bottle, please."

As the waitress jingled away, Deborah leaned her elbows on the table and announced, "I have a fun idea for a bridal shower game. We're going to have a contest to see who can hold their liquor the best."

"That's a bad idea," Claire said, shaking her head. "Like the Grinch stealing all the presents on Christmas Eve bad."

Ronnie groaned. "We're going to end up in jail again."

A cackle came from the crazy pregnant monkey at the end of the booth. "This is going to be so awesome!"

Chapter Two:
Rocking Around the Christmas Tree
Stripper Pole

Ronnie lifted the glass of amber-colored liquor, holding it out for a toast per her mother's insistence.

Once upon a time there was a girl who used to pay an obscene amount of money to have her five-thousand-square-foot, Georgian-style house decked out for Christmas. Now that washed-up trophy wife could barely afford to pay the monthly rent at the Dancing Winnebagos RV Park for an ancient camper that was dry rotting under the Arizona sun.

Not that Gramps made Ronnie pay rent, since she worked part-time at her step-grandmother's campground store several times a week to cover the cost of room and board. But if money were required, she'd surely be struggling, no thanks to her ex-husband. Actually, Lyle was her *non*-ex-husband, since he'd still been married to a woman from Wyoming when he'd exchanged vows with Ronnie.

Anyway, this would be her first Christmas since her make-believe world went up in flames.

Ronnie clinked glasses with her sisters and mom.

Sure, she'd drink to that no-good, cheating bastard rotting behind bars. She nodded as she brought her glass to her lips. And while she was at it, she'd drink to the end of Mrs. Veronica Jefferson once and for all, and the beginning of a new and improved Ms. Ronnie Morgan.

She downed a mouthful of the cognac.

Gah!

Ronnie stifled her gag. She'd never been a fan of sweet drinks. Gin and tonic had been her favorite ever since college. She liked her wine extra dry and her beer hoppy and pale. That explained why this first gulp of cognac made her teeth ache and her tongue so heavy that she had to let it hang out of her mouth to breathe.

"What are you, a dog?" Claire asked and wiped off her mouth with her sleeve, shuddering as she set her drink down on the table. Wearing her brown hair pulled back in a ponytail and a faded Scooby-Doo "Ruh Roh" T-shirt, Claire looked ten years younger than Ronnie rather than two.

"Too sweet," Ronnie slurred while scrubbing her tongue with one of the flimsy napkins the waitress had brought along with their glasses and the bottle of cognac their mom had ordered.

"Such dramatics, Veronica." Her mother waved her off with a flick of the pink talons she called fingernails. "You need to grow a pair of balls, like Claire and me."

Claire did a double-take, her dark eyes widening. "Say what now?"

Ronnie sat up straighter. "I have balls, Mother."

Deborah held out her index finger and thumb pinched close together. "Tiny ones, maybe. Like the jingly balls on our waitress's Christmas tree nipple-warmers."

"Nipple-warmers," Claire repeated, chuckling, and then she shrugged. "That works."

A snort-giggle came from the end of the bench. "Mom said 'balls,' Claire," Katie said, reminding Ronnie of a teenage boy.

Claire shot a quick frown at their youngest sister. "Don't encourage her, nutcracker." She turned back to Deborah. "You know, Mom, maybe we should talk about politics and religion tonight instead of testicles."

Their mother tapped a pink talon against her glass. "A lack of big balls would certainly explain why it took Veronica so long to leave her money-grubbing twat hound."

Katie laughed out a series of loud honking cries, sounding remarkably like a peacock had crawled up her ass.

Claire did a triple-take before turning to Ronnie with her mouth hanging open. "Did our mother just say—"

"My balls are way bigger than yours, Mother," Ronnie said, her scowl encompassing both her mom and her middle sister. "Maybe even bigger than Claire's. You two don't know the half of what I've gone through since walking out on Lyle."

"What about me?" Katie took a sip from the skinny striped straw in her red Shirley Temple drink. "My balls are *huge*. Just ask Deputy Dipshit and Sheriff Harrison."

Claire pinched the bridge of her nose. "We will not be discussing the size of anyone's balls with the local law, Kate. Not tonight, not tomorrow, not ever."

"Prove it, Veronica." Her mother held up her glass of cognac, her gaze challenging.

"Prove what?" Ronnie scoffed. "That I can drink away my problems better than you? No, thanks, Mother. I've been there and back already. Don't try to drag me into that divorce pity pool with you."

Deborah's cheeks darkened. She raised one perfectly arched brow. "You've spent the last several months blaming me for your failed marriage when the truth is that you were too much of a coward to walk away from Lyle while you still had some pride left. How about you prove that you've finally grown a spine?"

Claire sucked air between her teeth. "That's the cognac speaking, Ronnie. Don't listen to her."

"Butt out and finish your drink, Claire Alice," Deborah snapped. "This is between Veronica and me."

"I think this is a bad idea," Claire sang under her breath.

"I'll show you all a pair of big balls," Katie grumbled in Ronnie's other ear. "You guys just wait and prepare to be awed."

Blaming me for your failed marriage … too much of a coward …

Damn it! Her mom was right on both counts.

Ronnie lifted her glass. "Getting drunk on cognac won't prove that I have a spine, Mother." She gulped the sweet liquor down, hiding her wince and holding in a slight gag. "But it will certainly help me tolerate your sugarplum fairytales tonight."

"Pa-rum-pa-pum-pum," Katie sang, rapping out the beat on the table.

Ronnie set her glass down next to the bottle of cognac. "Now pour me another."

Two refills later …

"This stuff isn't so nasty after all," Ronnie said, setting her empty glass down yet again. She wiped her mouth off with the back of her sleeve.

Deborah hiccupped, and then tittered, squeaking like a mouse that had been goosed. "That's what I've been saying all along, but did you listen to me? No. What does your mother know?"

"Am I drunk?" Claire asked, pointing toward the dancers on stage. "Or is Rudolph the reindeer trying to hogtie Santa with a rope of tinsel garland?"

"You're drunk," Katie told Claire, popping the maraschino cherry from her drink into her mouth. "But according to the waitress, Santa was a bad boy and he paid Rudolph extra to tie him up and whip him in front of everyone."

Claire cringed, covering one eye with her hand. "I hope you're happy, Crazy Kate. You've ruined Christmas for me."

"You've told me that five times already, crybaby." Kate set her empty glass down, waving toward their waitress. "And if you keep calling me 'crazy,' I'll hogtie you with garland, too, before the night's over."

"I'd have to be blackout drunk for you to hogtie me, because unlike Ronnie," Claire said, lowering her hand and using it to poke Ronnie in the shoulder several times, "I can hold my liquor."

"I can hold my liquor, too." Ronnie shoved her sister's pokey finger away.

Claire snorted. "Right. Your head is swaying already."

"That's because I'm dancing to the music. Who's singing this? Betty Boop?"

"It's Madonna," Katie said, singing along with the Material Girl's version of "Santa Baby."

"Betty Boop," Claire said, laugh-snorting into her glass as she tipped sideways into Ronnie. "Now that's funny."

Ronnie pushed Claire back upright, catching her sister as she began to tip the other way toward their mom. She moved her hand in front of Claire's face. "Okay, *Señorita Soberado*, how many fingers do you see?"

Claire closed one eye, focusing on Ronnie's hand. "Seven."

"Ha! You're wrong, you drunken floozy."

"No, I'm not."

Ronnie stared at her fingers, blinking as they went in and out of focus. "One … two … four … six … seven." Huh. Claire was right, there were seven fingers. "What in the hell?"

Katie giggled in her ear and then lowered her two-fingered peace sign she'd added to Ronnie's finger count. "Gotcha."

"Now who's the drunken floozy?" Claire bumped her shoulder into Ronnie's.

Deborah tittered. "Kathryn, stop messing with your sisters while they're drunk."

"Hey, I've been waiting for this moment for three long decades." Katie grabbed the bottle of cognac and refilled their glasses. "Let the good times roll."

Another glass later …

"And then your father …"

Ronnie groaned under her breath as her mother's voice droned on and on in a never-ending litany of her father's marital crimes.

Next to her, Claire banged her forehead on the table repeatedly, making the amber liquid in the bottom of Ronnie's glass quake from impact tremors.

On her other side, Katie was … gone.

"Hey, where'd Katie go?" Ronnie asked, interrupting her mother's rant.

Claire sat upright and covered her face with her hands. She peeked out at Ronnie from between her fingers. "She had to go to the bathroom."

"When was that?"

"I don't remember." Claire pulled her hands down her face, her eyes looking glazed. "Somewhere on the timeline between Dad's extra-long work trips to Alaska when we were in our trouble-filled teens and Mom's tiki-themed anniversary party that he missed due to his plane being

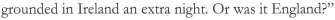

grounded in Ireland an extra night. Or was it England?"

"It was Scotland," Deborah corrected, her face pinched.

"Whatereverrrr," Claire slurred, then tried again. "Whatarevvv—" She licked her lips. "You know, one of those 'land' countries."

Ronnie looked out over the crowd of partially naked North Pole elves, scantily dressed "reindeer," and sweaty-faced Santas. The strobe lights turned the scene into a merrily macabre mashup, showcasing flashes of bawdy scenes that made her previous, drunken college revelries seem like tame bedtime stories.

She shuddered. Claire was right. Tonight would put a fair amount of tarnish on any Christmastime nostalgia for years to come.

She continued to seek out Katie in the froth of festivity, searching … searching … search—who was that?

Ronnie's gaze bounced back to the glasses-wearing Grinch sitting in a booth on the other side of the U-shaped stage. And by Grinch, she meant the green wrinkled face, poufy nose, swirly-tufted hair, and furry Santa hat. Holy Whoville! Somebody went way overboard on their costume for tonight's visit to the Nudie North Pole.

She squinted, trying to get a better look at him in spite of the strobes that lit up his large 1970s-style round glasses every couple of seconds. As she stared, he waved his long, furry fingers at her.

She gasped, sitting back against the bench seat.

He wrapped furry fingers around the bottle of beer on the table in front of him and lifted it toward her in a toast.

She slinked down into the seat.

His mouth widened in a gruesome smile, his teeth bright white under the strobe lights. He pointed at his glasses and then back at her.

I see you. Her mind played out the words in a growly Grinch voice.

Her heartbeat throbbed louder than the drum's bass pounding through the speakers. She needed to get out of here now!

She slid toward the end of the booth, only to be blocked by a body.

"Where do you think you're going?" Katie asked.

"I gotta go to the … to the bathroom. Yeah, that's it."

"You just went to the bathroom," Deborah said, sipping on her cognac. "Now slide back over so your pregnant-out-of-wedlock sister can sit back down."

"Nice, Mother dear." Katie sat down in the space Ronnie made, smelling like lavender and lemons. She must have used extra soap in the bathroom. "If you'll remember, I'm just following in your footsteps." She set an empty shot glass in the middle of the table.

"What's that for?" Claire asked, peering at it with one eye and then the other.

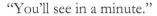

"You'll see in a minute."

Ronnie peeked around Katie. The Grinch was gone.

But not the bottle of beer. It still sat where he'd left it.

Crap. Where had he gone?

"I may have gotten pregnant with Veronica a little early," Deborah said, "but I quickly married your father. You, on the other hand, seem to be dragging your feet when it comes to Valentine." Deborah liked to address Kate's baby-daddy, Butch, by his legal name to keep him from thinking their relationship was getting too comfortable. It was the same reason why she called Claire's boyfriend "MacDonald" rather than just "Mac," like everyone else.

"I'm not dragging my feet," Katie said.

Deborah continued as if she hadn't spoken, "Which is just senseless, considering the amount of money your moonshine runner has in his bank account."

"There's nothing wrong with holding out on making any sort of commitment," Claire said, coming in loud and strong from Ronnie's right.

Claire had a fear of commitment that had kept her from settling down with one boyfriend, one job, one college major, or even one style of clothing for any length of time. Well, that was until she started working at the RV park and met Mac.

"First of all, Butch owns a legitimate bar," Katie said. "He doesn't run moonshine."

Deborah snorted. "That's right. Valentine has moved on to car swindling now."

"Butch is restoring old cars to be sold at auctions, Mother," Ronnie said, still searching for the Grinch in the crowd. "That's not a crime."

"Second, I'm not afraid of commitment," Katie said. "You have me confused with Claire."

"I'm not afraid," Claire grumbled. "I'm just a teeny tiny bit wary." She elbowed Ronnie. "You heard Mom's mile-long list of complaints about Dad. I just don't believe there is such a thing as wedded bliss." She lifted her empty glass in a mock toast toward their mom. "So why take the plunge and end up in the shitter for the rest of your life? Right, Mom?"

"Then what's taking you so long to marry that boy?" Deborah prodded, ignoring Claire's jab.

Katie shrugged. "I'm making sure."

Their mother gasped. "That he's the baby daddy?"

"No, Mom. Valentine is the father."

"Then what is there to make sure of, Kathryn?"

"None of your business." Katie poured more cognac from the half-empty bottle into their glasses. "It's time to start the next shower game."

"Which is what?" Ronnie asked, frowning at her once-again-full glass and the empty shot glass in the middle of the table.

"My own version of quarters. You guys have to take a drink every time I land the coin in the shot glass."

"But why do you get to be the only shooter?" Claire complained.

"Because I'm the sober one, knucklehead." Katie leaned forward and rolled the quarter down her nose. It bounced and landed perfectly in the small glass. "Now shush up and drink."

Several gulps of cognac later …

The Grinch was back. Actually, there were several of them now—some carrying drinks to and fro, some shaking their booties on stage, some howling at the dancers, and one sitting across the table from Ronnie.

She leaned over the table and squinted. No, wait. That last one was just her mother.

"Your hair is in my drink," Claire said with a slur that made "drink" sound like "shrink." She shoved Ronnie away, sending her leaning into Katie.

"I'm seeing Grinches," Ronnie told them after Katie set her back upright again, spotting a few more over by the bar.

Deborah pursed her lips and made a loud motorboat sound.

"Grinches? What's that supposed to mean?" Claire asked. "Is it code for something?"

"It means Ronnie is done drinking for tonight." Katie took Ronnie's glass of cognac and dumped it into Deborah's nearly empty glass.

"Ha!" Their mother cackled up at the ceiling. "I knew she'd lose."

Ronnie frowned at her empty glass, which wavered before her eyes. "I didn't lose. I'm just taking a li'l break."

"No, you lost." Deborah tapped her index finger on the table. "You lost when you married Lyle and you lost when he went to prison and you lost when the bank took your big fancy house and now you lost tonight at Dirty Gerties." She made an L with her finger and thumb, holding it up to her forehead. "You're a big loser, just like me." She hiccupped. "But that's okay, because we'll get our revenge on our ex-husbands. Just you see."

"I don't ..." Claire paused, shaking her head and then wincing. "I don't agree with any of that. And *feathermore* ..." She started to reach for her glass and froze with a wrinkled brow. "Did I say 'feathermore' or 'furthermore'?"

After several beats of the music had passed, Katie reached across Ronnie and nudged Claire. "Furthermore what?"

"I don't remember, but I need to pee."

Claire slid down in the booth like she was melting, dipping below the table and out of sight.

Katie jumped up, peering under the end of the table.

"Claire, what are you doing down there?" She reached under the table.

In a drunken blink, Ronnie saw Claire pop up on the outside of the booth, stumbling to the side a few steps while she wiped her hands off on her jeans.

Her face contorted in a cringe. "I think I touched a condom down there," she said and gagged … twice, which almost made Ronnie gag in sympathy. "I'll be back …" she gagged once more, "in a hot minute."

Katie watched her go with a worried brow. "Claire," she called after her. "If you're not back in five minutes, cold or hot, I'm coming to get you." She settled back into the booth. "Now where were we?" She picked up the quarter, lining up for her next shot. "Mom, if I make this, you need to *stop* drinking for the night."

"But it's my party."

"Too bad. You keep gulping drinks when you're supposed to just sip. You've had enough." As Katie started to let the quarter go, she looked toward the bar. "Oh, my— Son of a Christmas cracker! Claire! No!" She shot out of the booth.

Ronnie watched the quarter bounce once … twice … three times on the table before rolling off onto the floor.

Deborah laughed and downed her drink, reaching for the bottle.

Searching the crowd for her sisters, Ronnie saw the Grinch with the old-fashioned eyeglasses sitting at the bar. He waved once again, shooting her another one of those extra-wide, creepy smiles.

She scrambled toward the edge of the booth.

"Where do you think you're going?" Deborah asked as she emptied the last of the cognac bottle into her glass, filling it to the rim.

"I'm going to show you how big my balls are." Ronnie stood. Her legs were a tad shaky, but they held.

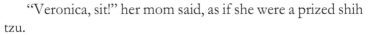

"Veronica, sit!" her mom said, as if she were a prized shih tzu.

"I'm not your damned show dog anymore, Mother." She saluted Deborah with a lot more slop than style. "Have a Merry Chrisss-miss Tree and a Happy Turkey!"

Without further ado, she aimed her feet in the direction of the bar and headed off to tell that Grinch to leave her and her family alone.

Or else.

An empty bottle of cognac later ...

"Why are my wrists tied together?" Claire asked, holding up her hands in front of Ronnie's face. A swath of silver tinsel garland was wrapped around both of her wrists and secured with a burly knot.

"I can't remember, but I think mine are, too." Ronnie held up her wrists. Sure enough, her bondage was the same as Claire's. She tugged on the garland, dragging Claire toward her.

Actually, she was tied to Claire. "How did this happen?"

She remembered a commotion over by the bar involving several Grinches, but not the one with the glasses, dammit. And she remembered someone dumping a glass of beer over a grab-ass Santa's head. But the rest was a strobe-filled blur.

"Where's the bridezilla?" Claire asked, nudging her chin toward the vacant seat on the other side of their mother's half-filled cognac glass. The empty bottle lay on its side in the middle of the table.

Ronnie lifted her bound hands so she could scratch her cheek. "I can't remember that either."

A wave of cheers and whistles hit her, knocking her head

back against the booth seat.

Claire shoulder-bumped her. "Look! Is that your mom?"

Ronnie's neck creaked like the Tin Man's sans a few squirts of oil as she turned to look at the stage. She searched the crowd of Grinches in Santa suits, their faces flashing in and out of focus with the strobe lights. "Where?"

"On stage. Rocking around that stripper pole."

Ronnie blinked several times, focusing above the crowd. "Yep, that's your mom."

"Oh, boy." Claire leaned over the table, pulling Ronnie's arms along with her. "She's really got a lock on that pole."

"Why is Katie dirty dancing with her?" Ronnie tried to pull her hands from their bindings with no luck. "Pregnant girls probably shouldn't be up on a stage. She might fall off."

"I don't think they're dancing," Claire sat back, her face covered in frowns from top to bottom as she watched the scene.

Ronnie's attention returned to the stage again as she tried to make sense of the commotion. "You're right. Katie isn't dancing. I think she's taking a ride on Mom's back." She smiled, her eyes growing misty. "It reminds me of when Katie was a little girl and she'd ride that pink hobby horse all around the yard yelling 'yee-haw' at any passerbys … or is it passersby? Or passersbys? Fudge nuggets, I can't ever get that one right."

Claire hooted. "Mom is like a bull. Look at her trying to buck Kate off."

"There are too many Grinches in here tonight," Ronnie murmured, scanning the writhing mass of red and white and green.

Claire let out a loud whistle, yelling out over the crowd, "Hold on, Kate! You've almost made it eight seconds!"

"I think they're after me," Ronnie told Claire. "They want to take me up to their creepy cave and lock me away forever."

A nudge came from Claire's direction.

Ronnie grunted.

Then an all-out shove knocked her sideways.

"What are you doing, Claire?"

"Kate needs our help. Come on, we can slide out together on your side."

Ronnie pushed back. "Katie said I'm not allowed to go near the Grinches."

She couldn't remember why, but she distinctly remembered her sister's face up close giving that order followed by an "Or else!"

"Grow a pair, Ronnie." Claire shoved her hard enough to send her tumbling out the end of the booth with Claire landing on top of her.

"Damn it, Claire. Get your elbow out of my cheek."

"Come on." Claire tugged her to her feet. "Let's go tackle Mom."

Another strand of garland later …

"I can't believe my own daughter tied me up while you two nincompoops just sat there and watched," Deborah said, her lower lip stuck out in a pout as she slumped in her seat across the table from Ronnie and Claire.

Ronnie's eyelids were getting heavy, along with her chin and her ears and the top of her noggin. The table beckoned like a soft, fluffy pillow.

"And how exactly were we supposed to help when our wrists were tied, too?" Claire slurred above the head-pounding beat.

"You could have snuck the knife from my purse and cut yourself loose so you could cut me free." Deborah sighed extra loud and long. "But like usual, I'll have to rescue me all by myself."

"What knife?" Ronnie asked, frowning at the girl Grinch on the stage who was taking off her Santa suit layer by layer. "Where's Katie?"

"She's over talking to the manager." Deborah rummaged in her purse for a minute and then pulled out a shiny black-bladed knife with a green handle. "This knife." She pointed it at Claire's bound wrists. "Scoot over here. I'll spring you so you can spring me."

"You're drunk, Mother. I don't think it's a good idea to play with a sharp knife around Claire." Ronnie took another look at the knife. Were those carvings on the handle? Was that real jade?

Deborah pooh-poohed Ronnie. "You have always been such a bore, Veronica, with your lists and day planners and loser husband. Now, come here, Claire."

Claire shifted toward their mom, tugging Ronnie along with her since they were still attached by the strand of garland.

"Where did you get that knife, Mom?" Claire asked.

"I found it at my new stepmother's house."

Ronnie cringed as their mother waved the sharp-looking blade toward Claire's hands. "It looks like black glass."

"I think it's obsidian," Claire said, leaning in for a closer look, almost touching her nose to the blade until Ronnie tugged her back. "Where was it in Ruby's house?"

"Down in her office behind some books on the shelf. Now hold still." Deborah eased the blade between the strands of garland and started sawing away.

The world swirled around Ronnie, the flashing lights blurring and slowing. Her eyes were so heavy. Something smelled like lemons and lavender. Maybe it was the garland.

"It's a very p-p-pretty knife," Ronnie said, letting her eyelids fall. "I think I'm gonna lay down now and take a li'l sleep."

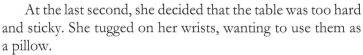

At the last second, she decided that the table was too hard and sticky. She tugged on her wrists, wanting to use them as a pillow.

Deborah gasped. "Dammit, Veronica!"

Claire groaned. "That looks like it's gonna hurt."

"What are you doing with that knife?" Katie spoke from high over Ronnie's head. "Oh, for God's sake! Is that blood?"

Chapter Three:
Santa Claus Is Coming to ~~Town~~ Jackrabbit Junction

Sunday, December 23rd

C laire Alice Morgan, will you do me the honor of becoming my wife?" Mac Garner asked aloud as he steered his pickup over the bridge into the Dancing Winnebagos RV Park.

He let those words sit out in the open for a few beats as he pulled up to the General Store, which was attached to the front of his aunt Ruby's house. Someone had woven garland and lights through the porch railing since he was here last, and hung a red-ribboned wreath next to the screen door.

The winter morning sunshine softened the splintered edges of the decades-old building, giving the aged wooden porch and siding a sort of romantic, Old West feel. Or maybe the warm, glowing effect was due to the rose-colored glasses he'd been wearing since he'd picked up *the ring* in Tucson.

The honor of becoming ...

What in the hell was he thinking? There was no way that

would fly with Claire. For one thing, it was a little too formal for a woman who wore a tool belt to work most days. For another, "my wife" had a possessive edge to it, like there would be ownership involved down the line. Asking her to marry him like that would make her drop her hammer and run clear back to South Dakota.

"Claire, will you consider spending the rest of your life as my wife?"

Crap. There was "*my* wife" again. And he didn't like how that rhymed at the end.

He sighed and shifted into park, watching the dust from the gravel drive drift off in the breeze.

Once upon a time, Mac had rolled along through life like a tumbleweed, bouncing here and there in the wind without a care in the world. Every so often, he'd get snagged on a pretty fence, but that never lasted for long, especially after he made it clear that his career as a geotechnician was his only true love, and then he would tumble along again sooner rather than later.

But eight months ago, he'd rolled into Claire. Her big brown eyes and tight T-shirts had snagged him from the start. Her soft lips and lush curves had kept him coming back for more.

One kiss wasn't enough.

One night in her bed wasn't nearly enough.

And he had a feeling that one lifetime with Claire wouldn't be enough, either, so he was going to do whatever he could to stay entangled with her for the rest of his years.

It was just his luck that she was allergic to commitment, especially the sort that included a vow and a ring.

He killed the engine.

He'd need to be careful when he proposed. Figure out how to word it just right.

He drummed his fingers on the steering wheel, clearing his throat. "Claire, please put me out of my misery and say you'll marry me."

Maybe, but the word "misery" was kind of negative, and Claire had enough pessimism in her life thanks to her mother. Mac shuddered at just the thought of facing off with Deborah repeatedly through the holiday. An abscessed tooth would have been preferable.

What about, "Claire, I'm gonna make you an offer you can't refuse."

He groaned. What was this, a *Godfather* movie?

Maybe if he just kept it simple: "How 'bout we get hitched?"

Christ, now he'd switched to *Beverly Hillbillies*. He just needed some of Granny's love potion to drug Claire and drag her off to a shotgun wedding.

Damn it. This proposing business could give a guy one hell of an ulcer.

He shoved open his pickup door, but didn't get out, taking a moment to enjoy a last breath of silence before heading into the storm of family theatrics that surely awaited him inside. With Deborah's ex-husband riding into town, Mac had little doubt that there would be plenty of fireworks lined up to blast off this holiday. He just needed to be careful so that nothing exploded in his face.

Another cool breeze blew past, carrying the scent of dried grass and the desert.

He stared out the windshield at the General Store's covered porch. A certain trouble-making beagle was lazing on his back at the top of the steps, basking in the mid-morning sunshine with his hind legs spread wide. One of the dog's front legs twitched.

Mac chuckled. Claire was right about her grandfather's prized pooch—Henry Ford wasn't much of a guard dog.

Claire …

Marriage …

He groaned again, looking down at his palms. They were

sweating already and he hadn't even left the cab of his pickup.

Scrubbing them on his jeans, he released a long, slow breath. He needed to sound cool and relaxed when he asked her, or he'd scare her off before he even showed her the ring.

"Claire, my life was a desert until you came along and watered it with your ..." He shook his head, not even able to finish that one. It was way too corny for either of them.

Leaning over, he opened the glovebox and pulled out the small box. The ring inside wasn't super fancy, just a small, heart-shaped garnet on a white gold band, similar to the ring Claire sometimes wore that had belonged to her grandmother.

He'd contemplated something bigger and more expensive with diamonds, but Claire really wasn't into jewelry. Accessories just got in her way while mending fences, fixing plumbing leaks, hanging drywall, and constructing new outbuildings at his aunt's RV park.

He stared down at the ring, turning it this way and that, making it sparkle thanks to the sun's rays.

"What's it going to take for you to make an honest man of me, Claire?" he asked under his breath.

Maybe he should start with her dad since he would be in town for a couple of days. Take the old-fashioned route and get his permission to ask for her hand in marriage.

He hadn't met Randy Morgan in person yet. The one time he'd traveled to South Dakota with Claire to pick up some of her clothes and other stuff, her father had been gone on a business trip, which wasn't unusual, according to her.

Mac had learned over the last few months from Claire and her sisters that their father had traveled for business during much of their childhood, missing several milestones in their lives. He wasn't surprised at their father's absence, though, being that Randy was a risk management consultant. Like Mac, their father often had to go out "in the field" to do his job, and often for weeks at a time.

However, in spite of Randy's traveling, each of the girls still had a strong bond with their father. Claire more so than Kate and Ronnie, because her mom had given up early on any hopes of molding her middle child into a mini version of herself. Although Deborah still liked to try to run Claire's life whenever …

The creak of a screen door opening made him look over at the General Store. Jess, his sixteen-year-old cousin, be-bopped out onto the porch in blue jeans and a Dancing Winnebagos RV Park sweatshirt, letting the screen door slam in her wake. Her red-haired ponytail bounced as she hopped toward Henry and reached down to scratch his belly, which earned her another leg twitch. Her freckled cheeks curved and she scratched Henry on the belly again, then she pinched her nose and shook her finger at the dog, saying something too quiet for Mac to hear.

Mac stuffed the ring back into his glovebox, burying it deep under some paperwork, a package of mechanical pencils, and a tire pressure gauge. The last thing he wanted was the local gossip queen, aka Jess, to see the ring. Otherwise, all of Jackrabbit Junction and a good portion of Yuccaville would know his wedding aspirations before he even made it inside the front door of the General Store.

He stepped out onto the ground. The slam of the pickup door drew Jess's gaze.

"Mac!" Her face broke out in a huge smile. "It's a good thing you're here already. We need your help real bad."

He stopped at the base of the porch steps. "What's wrong? Is your mom okay?"

"Yeah, but Claire's not."

He frowned. "What's wrong with Claire?"

"Well, for starters, last night was her mom's party and Claire stayed out *really* late."

Claire had mentioned the belated bachelorette-type party when he'd talked to her yesterday afternoon, but she didn't

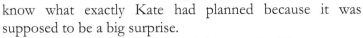

know what exactly Kate had planned because it was supposed to be a big surprise.

"Okay, so Claire's really tired this morning?"

"It's worse than that." Jessica lifted her hand to her mouth, miming drinking from a bottle.

"Oh. She's hungover."

Where had they gone to celebrate? The Shaft? That wasn't exactly a "big surprise," considering Kate, Ronnie, and Claire worked there most nights.

"Yeah, but it's even worse than that."

"Hell. She didn't get in another bar fight, did she?"

Claire had a history of swinging first and asking questions later. That was partly why Mac had started calling her "Slugger" shortly after they'd met. He'd hauled her out of a barroom brawl more than once, and he'd almost had to bail her out of another one when she'd gone up to South Dakota with Kate. Although Claire swore that her sister started that fight, and that she was only stepping in to help due to Kate being with child … and temporarily insane.

"I don't know, but a fight is not what I'm talking about."

He climbed the porch steps. "Damn it, Jess, spit it out."

"Fine, but you don't have to cuss about it."

When he growled and reached for her, she dodged and squealed.

Henry rolled to his feet and let out a yip of surprise. The old boy started to bristle, but then recognized Mac and instead rushed over to head bump his leg. The dog's hind end wiggled so hard that he almost fell down the porch steps.

"Jessica Lynn Wayne," Mac said, reaching down to scratch Henry behind the ears. "What's going on with Claire?"

She grimaced. "You should probably just come inside and see for yourself."

Chapter Four:
O Holy Night
Horrible

"What's she doing in the bathtub?" Claire heard Mac's voice faintly over the clanging of jingle bells in her head.

"We don't know."

Was that Jess?

"Harley found her there this morning when he got up to take a piss."

Yeah, that was definitely Jess. *Piss* was her favorite word lately. She kept finding new ways to use it that made Ruby gnash her teeth.

"Take a piss," Mac repeated. "You don't talk like that in front of your mom, right?"

"No. Unless I'm mad. Then all kinds of things slip out."

"Yeah," Mac said, his voice closer. "Same here."

Claire considered letting out a grunt or moan so Mac and Jess would know she was alive, but just thinking about using her throat made the back of her eyeballs hurt.

"Has she moved at all?" Mac asked.

"I don't think so, but the drool is gone."

"Drool?"

What drool?

"She had some dried on her cheek. Mom probably washed it off when she came to check on Claire earlier."

Oh, Lord. That was humiliating to hear in front of Mac. Claire would have blushed if it didn't hurt so much to push blood north of her neck at the moment. Instead, she decided to continue to play dead as she waited for her cognac hangover to truly finish her off.

Something rustled and then jingled overhead. Brightness on the other side of her eyelids followed. Mac must have drawn the shower curtain aside.

"How come nobody got her out of the tub?" Mac's low voice was right next to her now, taking some of the pain out of the cognac's lingering bite.

"Well, Mom and Harley and I talked about that, but Claire's not exactly light as a baby bird, you know," Jess explained.

Mac chuckled under his breath.

Claire contemplated grabbing something—a bar of soap would do—and lobbing it in the general direction of the bigmouthed teenager. But that meant moving several muscles at the same time, so she held her position as a curled-up corpse.

"And I'm not very strong," Jess added.

Maybe the girl's arms and legs weren't, but her jaw muscles could run non-stop for a week straight.

"Plus, Mom said her shoulder is sore from all of the tamales she's been making for Christmas dinner, and Harley didn't want to try because his broken leg is still healing."

Claire started to roll her eyes about Gramps's lame excuse but gave up that notion when a stab of pain pierced straight through to the back of her melon.

"We thought about hooking Henry up to Claire," Jess continued. "You know, like that poor little dog with the fake antlers that has to pull the Grinch's huge bag of stolen presents up the mountain? But late last night Henry chowed down half of Chester's plate of chili con carne while the old dudes were playing cards. Woo-wee! Who knew such a small, hairy butt could stink up a room so bad? Gramps tied him up outside on the porch before we all ended up in the tub with Claire. Mom and I had to escape to the kitchen until the room aired out."

Chester was one of Gramps's bristly Army buddies who lived at the RV park in a camper next to the old Winnebago Claire and her grandfather had driven down last spring before Mac, Ruby, and Jess were in the picture. Now Gramps was married to Ruby and Jess was his stepdaughter, which meant Claire's mom had a new stepsister, Claire had a new aunt, and …

Her brain hit the pause button on drawing out the new branches of her family tree. She had more important things to think about right now, like breathing in and out.

"So, you left poor Claire here to weather that smell?" Mac asked.

"Yeah. Truth be told she's sort of smelly, too. Like someone dipped her in a tub of alcohol, candy-coated her with cheap perfume, and then spritzed her with barf."

"Not mine," Claire mumbled between dried lips. She cringed at the loudness of her own voice.

"Good news, Jess." Mac's clothes rustled against the tub walls. Claire could hear laughter edging his voice. "Sleeping Beauty has awakened."

Jess snorted. "Good thing you didn't have to kiss her. With her stinking like the alley behind Naughty McKnob's in Yuccaville, you might lose your breakfast if you get too close."

The rustle of Mac's clothes stilled. "What were you doing in the back alley behind an adult toy store, Jessica Lynn?"

"Uhhhh, there was a stray cat that I was trying to catch while I was walking to Dad's hotel room after school."

Claire heard Mac grumble something not very nice about Jess's dad, and then he took her by the arm and tugged gently. "Come on, Slugger. Time to return to the land of the living."

"Don't want to," she mumbled, snuggling into the bunched-up towels under her head. "Everything hurts."

Mac didn't take no for an answer, lifting her under the arms until she was sitting upright in the tub—make that mostly upright. "Let's get you into the spare bedroom and … Claire, why are your wrists tied together with tinsel garland?"

"I don't want to remember." She opened her eyes to look down at her wrists, but then had to close one to stop seeing double.

"Is that blood on your shirt sleeve, Slugger?"

She opened the other eye and tried to inspect the dried,

dark red spots on her shirt. "I don't want to remember that either."

Mac carefully lifted her up and helped her out of the tub, brushing her hair away from her face.

He looked good this morning in a dark green flannel shirt that made his eyes more green than hazel. And he smelled even better. Fresh from the outside. Sun-washed and air-dried. His hair seemed lighter, too, but maybe that was thanks to the new LED lightbulbs she had installed in the bathroom last week.

He pulled her into a hug, kissing the top of her head. "Sweetheart, what happened last night?"

"Bad things." She shuddered against his chest. "Very bad things."

"Jess," Gramps hollered from somewhere in the house.

"I'm in the bathroom with Mac and Claire," Jess yelled back.

Claire flinched. Somebody needed to turn Jess's volume knob down several notches. Heck, turn the whole world down while they were at it. And shut off the lights for a bit longer, too.

Mac pulled back, lifting her bound wrists. "Is it your blood?" he asked, pulling up her shirt sleeves. His touch matched his tone, warm and gentle as he inspected the skin around her bound wrists.

Claire squeezed her eyes closed, replaying bits of what had happened. Bawdy images of sweaty-faced Santas, bouncing bazongas tipped with jingle ball pasties, and half-naked elves dancing around candy canes flashed through her thoughts, nauseating her all over again.

"No," she said, swallowing fast a few times. "I'm pretty sure it's Mom's blood."

"Is Claire awake?" Gramps's gruff voice in the doorway made her shoulders tighten. He needed to bring the noise down a level … *or five*, same as Jess.

"Yep, but she still stinks," Jess told him. "I think Mac should give her a good hose-down while she's in the bathtub."

Gramps snickered. "Probably a good delousing wouldn't hurt either." To Mac he said, "They were at Dirty Gerties last night, and according to Chester, it was a full house."

Claire scowled. How did Chester know about North Pole Nudie Night? Had he been hanging out there flirting with the owner again?

"Dirty Gerties?" Mac hit Claire with raised brows. "You were at a strip club for your mom's party?"

Jess's jaw gaped. "Oh my God! Were there naked people there and everything?"

"Yeah." Claire swayed again, clinging to Mac's shoulder. "And too much of *everything*."

"Hey!" A tinny, high-pitched voice came from behind Gramps.

Who did he have tucked away back there? Jiminy Cricket?

They all looked Gramps's way. "Oh yeah." He pulled a phone from his back pocket. "Katie's on the line. She wants to talk to Claire."

Claire shook her head when Gramps tried to hand her the phone, pointing to Mac. "Give it to him." She lowered her butt onto the edge of the tub.

"Why am I talking to Kate?" Mac asked, taking the phone and sitting next to her.

"Put her on speaker," Claire instructed, adding a "please" and holding her head in spite of her bound wrists.

He punched one of the buttons and held the phone toward her. "Talk away."

"Claire?" Kate said too loudly.

Claire jerked away from the phone. "What?"

"Are you alive?"

"Barely." She held up her hands as if Kate could see them. "Why are my wrists tied with tinsel garland, Kate?"

"For the safety of the residents in Yuccaville," her sister shot back.

"Real funny, spudnut. Whose blood is on my sleeve?"

"A three-hundred-pound plumber named Bluto who you decided needed an etiquette lesson."

"What?" Mac asked, his eyes widening. "You didn't get in another bar fight, did you, Slugger?"

Jess gaped while Gramps scowled.

Bluto?

"I don't think so."

Several more nausea-inducing images skipped through Claire's memory, starting with one involving a Santa sans pants, then jumping to a sexy North Pole elf spraying the crowd with a dildo glitter gun, and ending on more hooters with bouncing jingle ball pasties.

She covered her eyes, trying to make the sordid flashes go away. "So many boobs," she complained behind her hands.

Jess giggled again.

"I don't remember anyone named Bluto," Claire told Kate, still hiding behind her hands.

"That's because there was no Bluto," Kate said, snorting in laughter. "It's Mom's blood on your shirt."

"That's what I thought."

"She accidentally cut herself last night at the table and you tried to help her, only you two made a big mess before I could get the first-aid kit from behind the bar."

Mac looked away, a smile trying to round out his lips in spite of his obvious attempts to quell it.

Claire lowered her hands. "Why did I wake up in the bathtub?"

"Because I was going to steal your kidneys to sell on the black market," Kate said. "But I changed my mind due to it being Christmas and all."

Mac laughed at that, grunting when Claire elbowed him.

"You left your sister asleep in the tub," Gramps said, this time his scowl aimed at the phone.

"I had to."

"Katie," Gramps warned, undoubtedly getting ready to go into a full-blown lecture.

"I swear, Gramps. At first I put Claire in her bed," Kate explained. "But she said the room was spinning and she might throw up, so I moved her to the bathroom."

Claire grunted. "And then what? You just left me here in a cold, hard tub?"

"Sheesh, you want some stinky toe cheese with that whine?"

"I'm going to cram my stinky toes in your—"

"You didn't expect me to babysit you all night, did you?" Kate scoffed. "I made you a nice pillow out of Ruby's fluffiest towels, which I think was pretty darn nice of me considering you still sort of smelled like Santa puke."

"Santa puke?" Mac leaned away from her. "Please tell me that's just a random holiday-flavored comparison."

Claire shuddered. Honestly, she couldn't quite remember if there had been a vomiting Santa or not thanks to the cognac taking the sleigh reins after her mom cut herself. Nor did Claire remember leaving Dirty Gerties, riding back to Jackrabbit Junction, or being dumped in the tub, so she must have been really out of it by then. But she did have a cloudy memory of something about Ronnie and a bunch of Grinches.

"Besides," Kate continued her rebuttal. "I had Ronnie and Mom in the car yet. At least I didn't leave you in the condom-littered alley behind Naughty McKnob's."

Mac's focus whipped to Jess. Claire looked toward the teenager, too.

With a fake smile way too big for her freckled face, Jess backed out the door. Her footfalls thudded down the hallway as she made her escape before further questioning could take place.

"If you're done bitching and moaning," Kate continued. "You need to get your butt to The Shaft."

Claire leaned into Mac, thinking about how soft their bed was. "I don't think I'll be much use serving drinks for a few more hours at least." She'd need several gulps of chalky antacid and a Christmas miracle to stand upright while balancing glasses of liquid on a tray anytime soon.

"I don't want you to come help at the bar, you hungover hairball."

Glaring at the phone, Claire huffed. "Why do I have to come to the bar then, *Crazy* Kate?"

Silence came from the line for several seconds. Then in a cackling, scratchy voice, Kate said, "I told you last night to stop calling me that name, remember? Why do you think your wrists are tied?"

Claire exchanged a frown with Mac. "I'm not sure why my wrists are tied, not-crazy Kate. Things are pretty mixed up in my head."

"Well, let's hope for the sake of your currently gum-free hair that your brain straightens things out on your way here."

"If you put gum in my hair, Preg-zilla, I will hold you down and tickle you until you pee your pants, which won't be hard these days."

"Look how you talk to me after I took such good care of you last night. I should have left you up on that stage."

What stage? Another flash of lewd images rippled through her memory, making her flinch. Oh yeah, that stage. "Why do I have to come to The Shaft right this moment?"

"Because Dad's going to be here soon."

"Oh." Claire looked at her grandfather, whose gaze narrowed into a flinty glare.

With Gramps's ex-son-in-law in town, his daughter's head would likely explode and then acid rain would fall over the land. Joy to the world and all of that happy family holidays jazz.

"But first," Kate continued, "You and Mac need to go get Ronnie and bring her with you."

Go get Ronnie? At Grady's place? "We're not driving clear to Yuccaville to get Ronnie. Tell her to catch a ride from her boyfriend in one of the county's paddy wagons." Their dad needed to meet Grady anyway, same as he did Mac and Butch, even if Ronnie was trying to keep the sheriff at arm's length.

"Ronnie is not in Yuccaville."

"You didn't leave her at the sheriff's?"

"No, she was rather adamant about Grady not seeing her like *that*."

Mac frowned at the phone. "Like what, Kate?"

"Uhhhh …" There was a breathy pause, and then, "Mac, just go get Ronnie and drive my sisters here ASAP."

"Kate," Claire growled. "Where did you leave our sister?"

"Where do you think? I left her passed out in bed."

Chapter Five:
How the Grinch Stole ~~Christmas~~ Ronnie's Underwear

R onnie sniffed. Something smelled oddly familiar, spurring a long-faded memory from her childhood. Something to do with her mom …
She lifted her head from the pillow long enough to sniff again, keeping her eyelids tightly closed to block the bright light trying to burn through to her eyeballs.

Yep, she knew that smell from before … flowery sweet, yet smoky this time, too. Sort of like her mom's perfume mixed with cigar smoke. Her mother must have paid a visit to Gramps's Winnebago.

She cringed. Dang it, her mom and Manny had better not have used this bed for one of their kinky love romps.

Ronnie faceplanted into the pillow, groaning. A dull ache was chipping away at the inside of her skull. Never, ever, *ever* was she going to drink cognac again, no matter how much her mom taunted her.

Trying to ease the tension in her neck, she breathed slowly through her nose, like she did during her yoga routine.

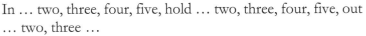

In … two, three, four, five, hold … two, three, four, five, out … two, three …

The pillow smelled, too, actually. Not just the room. A blend of hairspray and something musky, more manly. Her mom had definitely been in this bed.

Nutcrackers! Why couldn't the horny newlyweds stay in their own RV? First thing Ronnie was going to do—after she could sit up without falling over—was wash the bedsheets. And the comforter. And the curtains, too. And then she'd shampoo the carpet and wash down the walls.

But first, a bit more sleep until her headache eased …

She rolled onto her back, sinking into the mattress. Odd. The bed was cushier than she remembered. Then again, she had been spending a lot of nights in Grady's bed lately. Maybe she'd forgotten how the queen bed in the Winnebago felt. Or maybe Goldilocks had come along and added a foam pad to make the mattress feel "just right."

Like how she felt about Grady.

Actually, the sheriff of Cholla County was more than "just right," and that was becoming a problem for her.

The last thing she'd wanted to do when she'd escaped to southeastern Arizona was fall for anyone, especially someone with a shiny badge. She'd seen too many damned badges when her world crashed down around her ears thanks to her ex-husband's addiction to blondes, booger sugar, and dirty money.

She didn't even want to think about the sticky web she was snared in thanks to Lyle. Stealing cash and jewels from big-money crooks was bad enough, but tattling on them to the FBI was downright suicidal. If she ever saw her piece-of-shit ex again, she'd …

She huffed, and then returned to breathing in for five, holding for five, and releasing.

But then Grady had come along. Big, strong, protective. All wrapped up in a handsomely wrapped package.

Unfortunately, he also came with a sheriff's badge pinned to his chest and a reputation to protect. Therein lay half of her problem. With her checkered history, being associated publicly with Grady could be detrimental to his career.

The other half of the problem was the fact that after being royally fucked by Lyle on multiple levels, and still dealing with the nuclear fallout of her marriage, she'd vowed never to trust again, let alone allow her heart to stick out its head only to be blasted to smithereens. But night after night, she crawled willingly into Grady's bed, telling herself that this would all work out, and daydreaming that she could be a good little wife once again.

Deep inside, Ronnie knew better. Her good little wife days were history. And eventually, her nights with the sheriff would be, too. But until that day came, she couldn't help herself.

She stretched, sliding her feet along the satin sheets. They were so soft. Slipperier, too, than the cheap flannel sheets that were usually on Gramps's bed, with none of the scratchy pilling.

She yawned. How long could she get away with hiding out in the Winnebago today? Even though she was looking forward to seeing her father after months of being away from him, she was wringing her hands about what he might think of Grady.

Her mother had certainly trumpeted her disapproval after finding out on Thanksgiving about Ronnie dating the sheriff, and over the last few weeks none of Grady's attempts to charm Deborah had changed her mom's opinion on the matter. Ronnie had told him repeatedly that her mother's goodwill didn't amount to a hill of beans, but the poor guy refused to quit trying to melt the ice queen's heart.

The sound of footfalls on the gravel outside the RV made Ronnie grow still.

Somebody was coming.

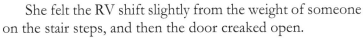

She felt the RV shift slightly from the weight of someone on the stair steps, and then the door creaked open.

She opened her eyes and sat up.

Too fast.

She tipped sideways, a dizzying wave sending her keeling over, back onto the bed.

Moaning, she blinked and tried to focus on the bold fuchsia-colored satin sheets.

Huh. Weren't these her mom's favorite sheets?

Her gaze shifted, focusing on the cute pink heart lights draped in a W along the top of the curtains.

Red. Velvet. Curtains.

Oh no!

Ronnie tried to push up onto her elbow, noticing the silver tinsel garland still wrapped loosely around one of her wrists.

Why do I have … A memory of Katie tying both of Ronnie's wrists in garland flitted through her head, followed by a flash of Claire's similarly bound wrists, some weird black and green knife, and blood.

Ronnie's gaze moved to the nightstand where a crystal light with a red-feather shade sat next to an empty bottle of cognac and a tube of something called *Caribbean Love Rub*. A big red set of neon lips glowed on the wall above the bed.

Oh, please no!

She struggled upright, her gaze darting around the room. Shit. She wasn't in Gramps's Winnebago. This was Manny's Airstream.

A purple silk robe had been hung on the back of the bedroom door. In the full-length mirror secured on the wall next to it, Ronnie caught sight of her reflection. Her hair was a snarled mess on one side and flat as a pancake on the other. In the bright morning light, her skin looked ghostly pale. Her eyes appeared sunken into her skull thanks to the dark half-circles under them.

Fortunately, Katie had brought her here instead of Grady's place. But how in the hell had she ended up in her mom's and stepfather's bed?

Something didn't make sense here. What had happened last night after she made it back to the Dancing Winnebagos RV Park?

A dull thud came from the other side of the bedroom door, followed by a *clang*.

Who was in the camper with her?

She crossed her fingers it was Claire out there making coffee for them both. Then they could laugh off the cognac nightmares and try to forget all of the nearly naked North Pole villagers and creepy waving Grinches at Dirty Gerties.

Whoever was on the other side of the bedroom door cleared *his* throat.

She glanced at the pillow next to hers. It had wrinkles and a head dent. That was Manny's side of the bed, wasn't it?

She gulped.

Who had been in bed next to her last night?

Ronnie looked down at her black sweater—the same one she'd had on last night. At least she was dressed … but wait! Her bra was missing.

She moved her legs again. The sheets were soft. Too soft. Slowly, she lifted the covers.

She groaned. Where were her jeans? More important, where was her *underwear*?

Son of a glitter gun! She had no memory of taking them off; but then again, she had no memory of climbing into this bed.

What in the hell had happened last night?!!

Someone rapped lightly on the door.

Her breath logjammed in her chest. She pulled the covers clear up to her chin.

"Who is it?" she called, cold with dread.

Please be Grady. Please be Grady. Please be Grady.

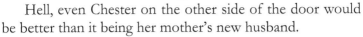

Hell, even Chester on the other side of the door would be better than it being her mother's new husband.

The knob turned.

The door inched open.

It wasn't Grady, nor Chester, nor Gramps.

Manny, her stepfather, stood in the doorway wearing her mom's pink robe with furry cuffs. His bare, hairy legs stuck out under the knee-length hem. The end of the bed blocked the rest of his ensemble.

"*Buenos días, mi amor.*" Manny smiled, holding up a cup of steaming something. His salt and pepper hair looked darker in the shadowed room, along with his eyes and mustache, making the Don Juan–wannabe look a decade younger. "I can't believe what happened last night."

Ronnie's ears clanged, her conscience sounding a death knell. *Holy jingle bell hell, what have I done?!!!*

Easing farther into the room, Manny frowned at the head-dented pillow next to her. "*Ay yi yi.* We probably shouldn't tell your mother about this when she sobers up."

Her heart keeled over, and then her brain jumped ship and began to sink into the murky depths of self-loathing.

"About what?" she whispered, her whole body locked in one big cringe.

His brown-eyed gaze met hers. "Don't you remember the little trick we played last night?"

She prayed that this "trick" didn't have anything to do with her missing underwear.

"No," she said. Actually, it came out more like a gasp. "What happened in here, Manny?"

His forehead crinkled. "You mean before or after the Grinch stole your underwear?"

Chapter Six:

It's a ~~Wonderful~~ Life
Preqosaurus Rex

The Shaft sat dark and quiet in the still morning air, like a stage waiting for the actors to show up and start running through their lines while the backstage crew double-checked the lighting and mics. Front and center—and alone, Kate sat on a barstool frowning at the door … waiting.

All she did these days was wait.

She waited on customers who were thirsty for something to take the edge off the world.

On Butch periodically to head out on or return from his latest classic car expedition.

On her sisters to stop being big scaredy-cats and go on the hunt for trouble instead of hiding from it.

On her mom to stop drinking so much and accept her part in the death of her thirty-five-year marriage.

On her dad to explain why he'd turned to another woman rather than end his loveless marriage first with his dignity intact.

On Deputy Dipshit to come up with another bullshit

reason to throw her in jail.

And on the baby in her womb to finish growing all ten fingers and toes so she could be done being a Pregosaurus Rex and get on with her new life as a mom.

Although truth be told, parenting scared the bejeezus out of her. Her two close-up, life-long examples of parenthood had taught her that raising kids was not only hard, but that staying in love with a partner through it all would be even harder.

Kate stared down at her ragged fingernails, pondering Butch's and her future. If she turned into her mother over the next few years, he might follow in the footsteps of her father. She knew how that story ended—and the cognac-guzzling shrew did *not* live happily ever after.

She sighed and checked her phone—still no messages from anyone, dammit, and it'd been thirty minutes since she'd called Claire to pick up Ronnie and get their butts over here. What was taking them so long? The RV park was only a hop, skip, and a jump up the road.

Her focus zeroed in on the bar and the jade knife partially wrapped in a bar towel laying in front of her.

She'd confiscated the weapon from her mom last night,

stuffing it in her purse before anyone else in Dirty Gerties caught sight of it and word got out around town. The last thing Kate and her sisters needed was to give Deputy Dipshit his next reason to lock them up again. He'd drool at the opportunity, probably throw together some cockamamie charges about stolen loot.

Kate leaned her elbows on the bar, wondering if Butch would show up before her sisters. She'd left home earlier than usual, telling him she wanted some time alone before they opened today to prep mentally for her father's arrival. He'd eyed her for a few seconds, his forehead lined, but then gave her a kiss good-bye and headed for the shower. He was none the wiser about the text her dad had sent before dawn saying he was running late—as in a whole day late, which was a fact she planned to share with her sisters as soon as they dragged their sorry butts here.

She tapped her fingers on the bar. Waiting and waiting.

Wanting to be alone for a bit this morning wasn't really a lie, but she'd left out that her mental "prepping" included researching the possible history of a certain kind of knife on Butch's office computer. From what Kate could find during her internet search, it was highly likely that a Maya artisan had meticulously crafted the jade handle a thousand years ago or more, and then used tree resin to seat the sharp obsidian blade into it. Amazingly, the resin was still holding, thanks in part to the dried and hardened strip of leather helping to secure the junction.

Kate peeled back the bar towel, staring down at the jade handle under the overhead bar lights. The carving looked worn, as if the knife had been put to good use, but maybe the crafter had smoothed the stone on purpose.

Once upon a time, knives like this were used by the Maya priests and kings during their bloodletting ceremonies. Kate had skimmed several articles about these types of rituals, which they would perform on their enemies, their own

villagers, and sometimes even children as sacrifices.

She leaned closer, shining her phone's flashlight on the handle. She needed a good magnifying glass to really see the details of the two figures carved there, but the scene seemed to depict one of these bloodletting rituals, showing the pricking of the flesh. Or, rather, the slicing of the prick, judging by the way the guy with the headdress was pointing a blade at the loincloth of the other guy.

Did the Maya wear loincloths? Or was it more like a longer kilt made of fur and feathers? It didn't really matter now, but she'd bet everyone went commando under whatever they wore back then. Ronnie would have fit right in with the Maya. Kate chuckled under her breath. Especially after last night.

She sat back on the stool. What did matter was where this blade had come from before it ended up in Jackrabbit Junction, Arizona. Since her mom claimed to have found the knife down in Ruby's basement office, it was probably one of Joe Martino's infamous, illicit skims. But skimmed from whom. And when?

Was it from an archaeological site, stolen to be sold on the black market? Had it been taken from a private collection somewhere south of the border? Was it brought over the border by a "mule," or a pair of them, like those two troublemakers from the university crew staying at the campground last fall? Or had it been stolen from a museum and Joe managed to pilfer it from the thieves?

Kate huffed. She'd love to string up Joe Martino and his sticky fingers, but since Ruby's old husband was already dead, that would do nothing for Kate besides landing her in jail for grave robbing and desecration of a human corpse.

Grave robbing … what was the penalty for something like that these days?

She grimaced. *Don't go there.*

Anyway, it was because of Joe's history of stealing very

expensive bits and pieces from the illegal shipments that he'd "moved" through this dusty corner of the country that had Claire jumping at her own shadow these days. It wasn't enough that the jerk put Ruby and Jess in danger when he was alive, but now Kate's family was in the picture, and she was damned well not going to wait around for …

The crunching of tires outside on gravel drew her gaze toward the door.

Was that Claire and Ronnie?

Or Butch?

Or Sheriff Harrison? Hell, Grady had probably sniffed in the wind and smelled that Kate had stumbled across more of Joe's felonious past.

She wrapped the knife back up in the bar towel and stashed it in her purse behind the bar. She was straightening her button-up work shirt as the door swung open.

Butch strolled inside, stopping when he saw her. The door eased closed behind him with a soft *thwap*.

Freshly shaven and showered, Valentine "Butch" Carter still made her libido purr with his long, lean frame and charming smile. Part suntanned cowboy, part easygoing drifter, all wrapped up in cool confidence. Kate hadn't had a chance at keeping her head or heart from swooning since the first time she'd crashed into him—well, into his pickup.

"Here I am, gorgeous." Butch's arms spread wide, matching his grin. "Now, what are your other two wishes?"

She rolled her eyes and returned to the barstool to wait some more, tapping her fingers on the bar. "The first wish would be for sexier pregnancy clothes. I highly doubt the jeans I bought last week will be sparking many parties in your pants once I'm bulging out over that elastic waist."

Chuckling, Butch came over and wrapped his arms around her from behind. His hands spanned her growing belly. "Sweetheart, you're—"

"Don't say that I'm having your child and it's incredibly

sexy, because I'm not buying that line of crap. I'm going to be waddling around soon with a beachball for a stomach and toes swollen up like sausages."

"Mmmmm, I love sausages."

"My hair is getting wavier, too, and wiry. Have you noticed that?"

He nuzzled her hair. "It smells sexy."

"It smells like my coconut-scented shampoo, same as always." She giggled as he sniffed behind her ear, tickling her. "If this keeps up, my hair will look like I stick a bobby pin in a light socket every morning."

"Electrified hair is hot."

She laughed. "Right, smoking hot."

His lips brushed her temple. "You'll look like the Heat Miser on that old Christmas special, *Santa Claus Is Coming to Town*."

"That's not good for you. The Heat Miser is always pissed off."

"Yeah, but it will be cute when you stomp your feet and curse at me for knocking you up."

She growled at him, leaning back into his warmth.

"And what's your second wish?" he whispered in her ear.

She bit her lower lip. "That my dad and you get along."

"I told you before, I'll get along just fine with him … unlike your mother." In spite of his soothing voice, she could feel the slight tension in him at the mention of her mom. "I have yet to meet another guy with whom I couldn't find at least one thing in common."

"And what do you think you'll have in common with a man who assesses risk day in and day out?"

He tipped her head back and smiled down at her. "My future stability with his hot-headed daughter." Then he dropped a kiss on her forehead and rounded the bar, pouring himself a glass of water from the tap. "What do I need to do to open?"

"Hit the lights and crank up the jukebox."

His smile flatlined. "You didn't mop, did you? You know that's not good for your back right now."

"I only mopped a little."

"Kate, I told you I'd do all of the mopping from now on, as well as anything that requires bending, twisting, or lifting." He winked at her. "You can keep gyrating and shimmying, though. And shaking your booty, too."

"You know I'm still a fully functioning woman."

He chuckled. "Yeah, that's one of my favorite things about you, especially when you function in front of me in just your lacy panties and that see-through bra." His gaze dipped to her chest.

She snapped her fingers in front of her face. "My eyes are up here, Valentine."

His gaze lifted, his expression shifting to stern. "Seriously, let me take over the more strenuous jobs, Kate. I don't want anything to happen to you or the baby."

She sighed. "Butch, I'm pregnant, not a Ming vase. You have to let me do my thing, or I'm going to go freakin' nuts waiting around for this kid to pop its head out." He opened his mouth, but before he could get a word out, she pointed at him and added with a hard squint, "And don't you dare even mention the word 'crazy' around me, or I'll slice your babymaker with an obsidian blade and offer your blood to *Yum Cimil*."

He paused with the glass of water midway to his mouth. One eyebrow inched upward. "Who?"

"The Maya god of the dead."

"That's a disturbing notion." He took a sip of water and set the glass down on the counter, eyeing her the whole time. "How long have you been thinking about bloodletting and me at the same time?"

"That's not important."

He snorted. "It sort of is."

"I'm just tired of everyone around here using the C-word with my name, and as fond as I am of ..." she glanced down toward his belt buckle ... "Captain Winky, I need to establish some ground rules going forward."

He shook his head, his expression pained. "I thought we agreed that you'd stop calling it pirate names."

"You don't like Long Dong Silver?"

"No."

"Private Peter Turgid?"

"No. Nor do I like Scurvylegs McBoner or Ol' One-Eyed Willy."

"How about 'who-hoo dilly'? That has a nice ring to it."

"Who-hoo what?"

She held up her index finger. "Better yet, pink torpedo."

"That sounds like something they'd say in a porno flick."

"Your tinkle-toy?"

"There are too many reasons to *never* say that again."

"Left-handed banjo?"

A deep V formed on his forehead. "I'm not sure I get that reference."

"Hobnocker? Thunder stick? Love cannon?"

He laughed, holding up his hand for her to stop.

"Fine, I'll stick to coming up with baby names for now, but promise me you won't call me 'crazy.' "

Still chuckling, he reached across the bar and took her hand. "I promise." He raised it to his lips and kissed her knuckles, sealing the deal.

"Good." She pulled free and palmed his cheek, losing herself for a moment in the warmth of his dark blue gaze.

"But I really like 'bad mama jama' for you," he said with a quick grin, and then he sang the rest of the chorus from the old 1980s Carl Carlton song to her: "Just as fine as she can be."

"No. Absolutely not."

A horn honked outside, followed by the crunching of

tires on gravel.

Butch went to the door, pulling it open a crack. "It's not your dad."

She scooted off the chair, joining him at the door. Her sisters had arrived, with Mac driving their chariot—aka Claire's green Jeep. "I forgot to tell you. Dad texted a bit ago to say he's not coming into town until tomorrow."

Butch frowned down at her. "Why not?"

"Something about needing to stop at a client's place near Santa Fe this morning to wrap up some last-minute paperwork." When he continued to frown, she waved off his look of concern. "It's no big deal, trust me. Dad always has and always will be busy, even on holidays."

"Maybe you should head home early tonight and start packing for our trip. Get that out of the way."

He'd mentioned her lack of luggage preparations yesterday afternoon, too. After claiming she was a fast packer, Kate had scurried into the bathroom to take a shower and get ready to pick up her mom and sisters for their Dirty Gerties party. She'd managed to avoid any additional talk about traveling to see his family until now.

"Yeah, about that ..."

The horn honked again.

Claire leaned out the passenger side window. "Kate! Get your ass in the Jeep!"

She slipped by Butch and stepped out under the wooden awning. Shading her eyes, she hollered, "Why? Am I going for a ride somewhere?"

"Yeah. You're coming with us."

"I can't go. We have a bar to open." Besides, Claire and Ronnie were supposed to be here to meet their dad per Kate's earlier call. Where were they going?

Mac stepped out of the Jeep, striding her way. "You need to go with them to get your mom, Kate. They need a driver. I'll help Butch open the place."

"Why do I have to go get Mom?" she asked Mac, holding the door wide for him.

The horn honked again.

Kate aimed a middle-fingered salute at Claire, saying to Mac, "After last night's drunkenfest, it's probably better to leave sleeping beauty be for twenty-four hours."

"You'll get no argument from me," Mac said, nodding a "hello" at Butch.

"Then what's Claire's problem?"

He rubbed the back of his neck. "Well, besides her nasty hangover, she and Ronnie can't find your mother."

"Can't find …" Kate frowned up at him. "I left her in her bed last night."

"Maybe so, but now she's gone, and your sisters have decided they need your help to find her."

The horn honked again. Twice.

"What are you waiting for?" Claire yelled from the passenger window. "Let's go, Crazy Kate!"

Butch sucked air through his teeth, wincing visibly.

Something snapped in Kate's head. A tidal wave of hot anger crashed through her, clear to her fingertips and toes. She screamed like a mad monkey in the direction of the Jeep. "Stop calling me 'crazy,' dammit!" She raced back into The Shaft, grabbed her coat and purse from behind the bar, and rushed past Butch.

He caught her by the arm, stopping her just over the threshold. "Don't sacrifice Claire to *Yum Cimil*, sweetheart." Butch gave her a quick kiss. "That would ruin Mac's Christmas."

She growled, hoisting her purse on her shoulder. "Fine, but if she keeps calling me 'crazy,' blood will be spilled. Mark my words."

Chapter Seven:
I Saw Mommy ~~Kissing~~ Santa Claus
~~Kicking~~

"Look at Katie's face." Ronnie let out a low whistle from the backseat of the Jeep. "She's breathing fire."

Claire stared out the windshield at the red-cheeked pregnant woman storming toward them across the parking lot. Kate's mouth moved a mile a minute as she glared at the Jeep.

"What do you think the hothead is saying?" Claire asked, grinning in spite of the dull pounding thanks to the hangover construction still going on in her brain. She pushed her sunglasses higher up on her nose to keep out more sunlight.

The pain reliever pills she'd taken after talking to Kate earlier had eased some of the effects of cognac still coursing in her veins, like the nausea and the aches in her wrists from being bound all night. A hot shower and even hotter cup of coffee had helped, too, along with a quick neck massage from Mac. But it was going to take a few more hours to fully return to the land of the living.

"I highly doubt she's reciting ' 'Twas the Night Before Christmas.' " Ronnie chuckled when Katie shook her fist at them as she rounded the front of the Jeep. "Knowing Katie's extensive knowledge of vulgar vocabulary, it's probably something that would make my virgin ears burn."

"Virgin?" Claire scoffed, glancing back at Ronnie, who was hiding behind her big Jackie O–style sunglasses. "Says the woman smelling like Mom's flowery perfume who woke up half-naked in our stepfather's bed."

Ronnie groaned, slumping down in the seat as Kate yanked open the driver's side door.

"I told you to stop calling me 'crazy'!" the Pregosaurus Rex screamed and slung her purse at Claire.

The leather bag hit her in the shoulder—hard—before tumbling to the floor at her feet. "Ouch!" She glared at Kate, who was settling in behind the steering wheel. "What the hell do you have in there?" She reached down and picked up the purse. "A frickin' boulder?"

Ronnie snickered. "It's an over the shoulder boulder holder." When Kate frowned at Jackie-Junior in the rearview mirror, Ronnie added, "You know, what Chester calls 'bras.' Only in this case, it really is an actual over the shoulder bould—"

"We get it, Cousin Eddie," Claire cut her off.

"Who's Cousin Eddie?" Ronnie asked.

Kate turned in her seat. "The dorky guy from *National Lampoon's Christmas Vacation*."

"Oh, yeah." Ronnie slapped Claire's shoulder. "I'm not a dork."

"I never said you were, your little sister did." Claire started to unzip Kate's purse to check out what was inside. The knocked-up nutter wasn't packing heat again, was she?

Last month, Kate had taken a shine to carrying an antique derringer Joe had skimmed. And it wasn't just any peashooter either. According to Grady, who'd looked into the gun's origins, the derringer had been stolen from a museum collection of items belonging to Pancho Villa, the legendary general during the Mexican revolution in the early twentieth century.

Kate snatched her purse from Claire's hands. "Stay out of there."

"Why?" She had gotten into Kate's purse many times in the past to borrow her phone or some lip balm or cash or whatever without Kate caring.

"There's nothing in there." Her sister's left eye twitched.

"Don't try to sell me one of your fairydiddles, Kate. What are you hiding now?" She reached for the purse, but Kate stuffed it down next to the driver's side door and then batted away Claire's hands. "Why won't you let me look in your purse?"

What had happened to that fancy knife their mom had cut herself with last night? Claire's memory of it was a blur, but she remembered something weird carved on the green handle. Was that what Kate had stashed away in there?

"Because it's Christmas and there could be a present in there. Now buckle up and explain this business with Mom."

Claire sat back, letting go of her suspicions for now.

"She was missing when Manny came to check on us this morning," Ronnie said as Kate started the engine.

"Missing since when? I left her next to you in the bed last night." She shifted into gear and hit the gas. "You two were tucked in tight, snug as bugs in a rug."

"I don't know when she left because that damned cognac knocked my legs out from under me."

"Same here," Claire said. "Only it kicked me in the gut a couple of times before leaving me curled up in a bathtub." She shot a sideways glare at Kate. "Oh wait, it was my loving sister who left me in a tub."

"Cry me a river, you big whiner-forty-niner. Better a tub than facedown in a toilet bowl like I've been for the last four months."

She had a point. One night of nausea was kid's play after the roller-coaster Kate had been riding since finding out she had a bun in the oven.

Ronnie sighed. "I barely remember walking into Manny's camper, let alone climbing into his and Mom's bed."

"You didn't walk. It was more like a series of lurches that ended with a faceplant into the mattress." Kate's cheeks rounded when she glanced in the rearview mirror.

"Hardy-har-har. What happened to my dang underwear, Katie?"

"Oh, I forgot." She dug into her coat pocket while tapping the brakes as they reached the point where the parking lot dumped out onto the road leading to the RV park. "Here." Kate held out a plastic baggie with a pair of blue panties wadded up inside for Ronnie to take.

Claire grabbed the baggie before Ronnie could. "We should wrap these up, slap a bow on them, and put them under the tree for Grady from his Secret Santa."

Kate nodded. "And we could set it up so he opens the gift in front of Dad. That would put good ol' Sheriff Big Britches dead center on the hot seat instead of Mac or Butch."

Ronnie leaned forward and snatched the baggie out of Claire's hands. "Leave Grady alone. He's had to deal with nothing but trouble and criticism from Mom since she found out we're doing the wild thing."

"Everyone is fair game for poking and prodding when it comes to Mom," Claire grumbled. She'd had a lifetime of experience with Deborah's censure on everything from clothing to men to careers. Her mother was a real pro at taking out her unhappiness in her own life on others—her version of living vicariously.

Claire pointed in the direction of the RV park. "Turn right."

Kate did as told. "She didn't take anyone's vehicle for a joy ride, did she?"

"Mom wouldn't know joy if it hit her upside the head with a bottle of cognac," Ronnie muttered.

"All vehicles are accounted for." Claire and Mac had made sure of that before heading to The Shaft to get Kate.

Ronnie leaned forward between the two front seats. "Manny knew well enough from dealing with Mom's drinking over the past month to hide his pickup keys before heading over to Gramps's Winnebago to sleep."

"That's kind of sad," Kate said.

"Not just kind of." Claire shifted, rubbing the tender muscles in the back of her neck.

Kate spared them both a glance as she steered toward the RV park. "By the way, Dad's not coming into town today."

"We know," Claire said. "He called when I was taking a shower. Jess took the message. He'll be here tomorrow morning and wants to spend Christmas Eve with us. Gramps didn't look happy at the news, of course, but maybe he was just grumpy about the sun shining today—you never know with him."

"True," Kate said. "But he seems happier overall, though, since marrying Ruby, don't you think?"

Ronnie harumphed. "I think he'd be all giggles and twirls if it weren't for Mom and her dark clouds hanging around day after day."

"Thankfully, Manny takes the brunt of her misery most of the time." Claire didn't know what their knight in shining armor saw in their mother, but she was grateful for him acting as a buffer more than she could say—which she told Manny often. "Mac looked relieved to have another day before having to meet Dad."

At least that phone call seemed to relieve some of the tension lines Claire had noticed around his mouth since he'd hauled her out of the tub. But there was a shadow still hovering behind his eyes when he looked at her, like he had something needling him. Until she could talk to him alone, she could only guess what might be buzzing in that big brain of his. Maybe there was a situation at work giving him grief.

She hoped he wouldn't have to go back to Tucson right away. They'd been spending too much time away from each other these days, which was part her fault since she didn't want to stay more than a day or two in the city while he worked long hours.

"Mom will be happy to hear Dad will be in town one day less when we find her," Ronnie said. "Now, why in the hell did you take my underwear, Katie?"

"Because you kept talking about wanting to go for a walk down by the creek to look at the stars, but Manny and I agreed that you were too wasted to go on a walkabout and I wanted to go home to my nice warm bed. At first, I just took your pants and hid them under the sink, but then you tried to go outside in your underwear."

"So you stole them?"

Kate's face pinched on one side. "I *kind of* stole them."

"Right off Ronnie's ass?" Claire asked, trying to picture the scene. There was a lot of leg kicking and foot thrashing in her imaginary version, ending with a black eye.

"Oh, no. Captain Commando here took them off on her own and threw them out the camper door. I just decided to pocket them and leave—after tucking her half-naked ass in next to Mom, of course."

"What! No." Ronnie's cheeks darkened.

Kate shot Claire a wry grin. "Actually, it was a whole naked ass. I think all of that yoga she's doing is paying off. I could've bounced a quarter off of her cheeks into a shot glass. It's no wonder Grady follows her around like a li'l lap law dog, drooling at her booty."

"Why would I do that, Katie?"

Claire glanced back at the yoga queen, chuckling. "Because you have an eager beaver in your bloomers now that you've seduced the sheriff of Cholla County."

"I did not seduce Grady." A smile played on the corner of Ronnie's lips. "At least not on purpose."

"I might've played a little trick on you last night," Kate explained. "Something I came up with right before Manny left to go sleep in Gramps's Winnebago."

"What kind of trick?" Ronnie growled more than asked.

"One involving a bit of reverse psychology when it comes to your previous prudishness from our younger years. I might have thrown a comparison to Claire in there, knowing in the past that you've wanted to be as free-spirited as she is."

Claire grimaced out the window at the wide-open desert. Make that *was*, Claire thought. Between falling for Mac and hiding amongst the ghosts of Joe's criminal past in Jackrabbit Junction, she tended to rein in her wild ways more often than not now.

"Free-spirited, yes," Ronnie said. "Bare-ass naked, no." After a beat of silence, she added, "You better not have taken any pictures of my bare butt."

"Why would I do that?"

"One word—blackmail. It wouldn't be the first time you've used that trick with me."

Kate aimed a scowl in the rearview mirror. "I was thirteen, Ronnie. I needed money. Besides, you were wearing your underwear in that picture, and he was your boyfriend at the time."

"You needed money for candy bars, you brat, not to live a dangerous life on the street." Ronnie poked Kate in the shoulder. "You're just lucky Claire was able to break into his truck and steal that picture back, or I'd have burned holes in all of your favorite sweaters."

Holding up her right hand, Kate said, "No pictures, I solemnly swear. Only a pair of blue underwear to sell online to the highest bidder, but lucky for you I don't need the money right now and Butch is keeping me flush in candy bars."

"You should have kept her blue undies to use as a 'Get

out of jail free' pass with Grady," Claire said as they rolled across the bridge over Jackrabbit Creek, which lined the western edge of the RV park.

Kate tapped the brakes. "Now where?" she asked Claire.

"Let's start at the General Store. See if Manny and Chester had any luck finding Mom in any of the bathrooms or the laundry building."

"And if not?"

Claire blew out a breath. "I don't know. I guess we go camper to camper until we find her."

"Manny mentioned calling Grady if they didn't find her on the first go-round," Ronnie said, chewing on her knuckle.

Kate shot Claire a worried brow. "You don't think she might have gone down to the creek, do you?"

"No. Mom is not a nature lover. The sand along the banks would get into her fancy pink princess slippers. Besides, the creek isn't much more than a trickle now since we haven't had rain in over a month."

"If I'd have known Mom would do this, I would have tied her to the bed." Kate pulled to a stop in front of the General Store. "Sorry, guys. I should have been more diligent. Does this mean I'm going to be a bad mother? I don't want to have to cage up my kid, but …"

Claire reached across and squeezed her shoulder. "Kate, Mom is an adult. You tucked her snug in her bed. Short of planting sugarplum visions in her head, you did your part in getting us home safe and sound. Thank you—even if the bathtub was cold and hard."

"You're going to be a good momma, Katie," Ronnie said, opening the backseat door. "But you could have left me my underwear on the nightstand."

"Where's the fun in that?" Claire asked, sharing a grin with Kate as they followed Ronnie up the steps onto the front porch.

"So, when did Manny see her last?" Kate asked.

Holding the door for them, Ronnie answered, "Last night when he left to go sleep in Gramps's Winnebago since I was in his bed with Mom. He came over this morning to grab some of his favorite coffee and check on us. That's when we realized she was missing."

Ronnie punched Kate lightly in the shoulder as she passed in front of her over the threshold. "Thanks to you, I about keeled over when he walked into the bedroom in his robe, and there I sat bare-assed. That's right up there with finding out the FBI had been watching those hidden camera videos Lyle took of me enjoying my extra-long showers."

Claire patted Ronnie on the head as she slid by her. "My big sister, the FBI's favorite porn star. What an honor it is to share blood with you."

"Zip it, you streaker." Ronnie closed the door behind them.

"What's the reason for practically hogtying Ronnie and me, anyway?" Claire asked as she trailed Kate across the empty store toward the curtain hanging in the doorway that led to the living area of the house.

"Don't you remember what you two did last night?"

"Uhhh, bits and pieces, but they are all jumbled together." Claire aimed a frown back at Ronnie. "Do you remember what I did last night to earn being wrist-bound?"

"I remember a bunch of Grinches everywhere. Everything else is hazy, same as you."

Kate pulled the curtain aside. "You don't remember Mom kicking that huge, beefy Santa Claus in the shin when he pulled you onto his lap and asked if you'd like a big candy cane for Christmas?"

"Now that you mention it." Claire cringed, remembering the scent of peppermint. "I do remember that, and being in a tugging match with Santa and Mom, only I was the rope."

"Bingo." Kate shook her head. "And that was the *second* time I had to pull you out of a kerfuffle. The first time you lost at arm wrestling to an ugly version of Mrs. Claus at the bar, only it turned out that the missus was really a mister who liked to wear women's bloomers. When you found out he'd misrepresented himself, you grabbed the stuffing out of one of his fake boobs, threw it on the floor, and stomped on it."

"Oh, crud. Right. Now I remember that, too." Only Claire wished she didn't. It would definitely not be on her list of finer holiday memories for future reminiscing.

"Jeez, Claire," Ronnie said, chuckling. "You were a hot mess last night."

"Says the girl who tackled a little old man, called him 'Grinch' several times, and then threatened to break his glasses," Kate said.

Ronnie made a small, pained sound in her throat. "I was having some Grinch issues last night."

"No shit, looney tune." Kate came to a stop in the middle of Ruby's rec room. "It's a good thing that old boy was extra lonely and thought of your harassment as foreplay."

"He did?" Ronnie asked, leaning back against the antique walnut bar that had come with the campground when Joe bought the place for Ruby way back when.

"Well, sure. Having a long-legged woman straddle him in the middle of a nudie bar and threaten to string him up by his cockles? You made his night."

"Who was Ronnie going to string up by his cockles?" Chester Thomas asked from the archway into the kitchen, looking extra bristly this morning from his short steely hair and his grizzled cheeks to his wiry chest hair poking out of his holey T-shirt. He had a piece of toast topped with what looked like chili beans in one hand and a steaming mug in the other.

"Never mind," Ronnie said, dropping onto a barstool. "Ugh. I'm never drinking cognac again."

Chester shuffled into the rec room, joining their merry memory making. "Next time you gals have a wild and woolly party at Dirty Gerties, you'd better invite me."

Gramps burst in through the back door, pausing when he saw the four of them. His face was lined with pain or worry, Claire couldn't tell which. "What's going on, Gramps?"

He snort-huffed. "I have good news and bad news." He thumbed back toward the door he'd just came through. "The good news is we found your mother."

Her sigh of relief made Claire realize she'd been holding her breath.

"What's the bad news?" Chester spoke up around a mouthful of beans and toast.

Gramps threw his hands in the air. "We can't get the damned mule-headed girl to come down."

Chapter Eight:
Up on ~~the Housetop~~ Where?

"How are you going to get her down?" Claire asked.

Ronnie frowned at her sister while zipping up her fleece vest. The sun hadn't quite warmed the breeze yet this morning. "What do you mean how am I going to get Mom down? Why is it *my* job?"

"Because you're the oldest," Claire said, shooting her a grin. "And, therefore, the wisest."

"And the tallest," Katie added, shielding her eyes.

The damned sunshine seemed about three times brighter than usual for Ronnie's hungover eyeballs. She scoffed. "That's a load of hogswallop and malollypop, and you two sugarplums know it."

It wasn't her fault that their mom had temporarily lost touch with solid ground—literally—and decided to plop her buns up on the rooftop of the newly built, single-story campground restroom. If anything, it should be Claire's job to bring their mother back to earth, since she helped to construct the concrete block building last month, including shingling the roof.

"You go up there and drag her down, Claire." Ronnie crossed her arms. "You're the one who built her roost."

"Yeah, but you minored in psychology in college. It's about time you put that to work on someone other than that paranoid woman in your mirror."

"I didn't minor in psychology. I took one abnormal psych class to fulfill my degree requirements." Ronnie aimed a squint at Claire. "And I'm not paranoid. I'm just a tad more guarded these days."

"Ha! The Queen of England is less guarded than you lately." Claire pointed toward the roof. "Refusing to come down from a bathroom rooftop is close enough to abnormal behavior for me. I nominate you to go up there and talk her back to earth."

Katie planted her hands on her hips. "I swear, both of your hearts are two sizes too small." She bumped Ronnie aside. "Move it. I'll go up there and get her down."

"Uh, no you won't." Claire caught Katie's arm and tugged her away from the ladder that was leaning against the side of the building. "No preggo-platypuses allowed on my roof." She pointed at Ronnie. "The two of us will go up together and bring her down."

Ronnie sighed. "Fine. But Katie should go get some chloroform just in case this goes south and strong-arming is required."

"I can hear you girls talking, you know," Deborah's voice floated down from overhead.

"Good," Claire hollered back. "That means your ears are working just fine. Now let's get the rest of your body moving down this ladder."

"I'm not coming down right now, Claire Alice. So just go away and leave me be."

"No can do, Prancer." Claire looked at Ronnie. "Ready?"

With a nod, Ronnie followed her sister up the ladder, taking Claire's hand at the top to help her onto the roof.

"You sure you don't want me up there, too?" Katie called up from the bottom ladder rung.

Claire glared down. "Positive. Now get your foot off that rung. Butch will chew us out if he hears we even let you touch a ladder."

"Valentine isn't the boss of me."

"Maybe not," Ronnie said, tag-teaming with Claire's glare. "But he's my boss, and I like doing his bookkeeping, so go sit over by that tree and wait for us."

"You two suck. I bet you wouldn't let poor little Rudolph join in any of your reindeer games, either." Grumbling, Katie clomped over to the tree, leaning against it as she scowled up at them.

Ronnie exchanged grins with Claire, but then she turned and saw her mother sitting near the apex of the roof, staring out at the desert valley behind a pair of dark sunglasses. A pink polka-dotted headscarf kept Deborah's hair in place in spite of the breeze. The lines on her face were more visible this morning, as if her shields were down. Her legs were drawn up tight into her chest with her folded arms resting on her knees. Enveloped in Manny's leather coat, Deborah looked smaller than usual, more vulnerable. More human than she had in years. It didn't take a class in psychology to see that her mom was not hanging out up here to keep an eye out for Santa's sleigh.

A pinch of pain twanged in Ronnie's chest. Tucking her hands into her vest pockets, she followed her sister over to their mom's perch.

"Okay," Claire said, arms crossed. "What's going on?"

Deborah shrugged. "Maybe I'm just enjoying the view."

"Are you still drunk?" Ronnie asked. "You really need to start taking it easy on the cognac."

"No, I'm not drunk. You think I would climb a ladder if I was?"

"I don't know, Mother. You haven't been the most

logical person since you came down to Arizona."

Deborah scoffed. "You try wasting over three decades of your younger, better years on a lousy marriage and see if you don't tilt a bit as you stumble away from its smoldering remains."

Having wasted a few good years on a lousy son of a bitch herself, Ronnie had an inkling of how much that stung.

Sighing, Claire sat down next to their mom and frowned out at the desert. "So, is this rooftop protest about getting older or about Dad coming for a visit?"

"Both." Deborah sniffed. "But mostly the latter."

A cool breeze ruffled Ronnie's hair. She tucked her shoulders in tighter and hunkered down onto the roof on the other side of her mom from Claire. It was warmer there with the asphalt shingles heating her buns through her jeans.

"Dad's only going to be here for a day or two," Ronnie said, watching a raven cruise the thermals over the small ravine that ran behind the RV park.

"With his girlfriend," her mom grumbled.

"Actually, he's coming alone," Claire told her. "Besides, you have a doting husband now, remember? So, you've one-upped him."

"Manuel is a good man," Deborah said, but there was a wistfulness in her voice.

"Manny is a great guy, not just a good one." Ronnie looked at her sister, who nodded and added, "And he has adopted us as his own family just as we are, not expecting anything more."

"He's a wonderful lover, too," Deborah said, a hint of a smile on her lips.

Ronnie cringed, while Claire covered her ears and sang, "Jinglebellsjinglebellsjinglebellsjinglebellsjinglebellsjing—"

Deborah yanked one of Claire's hands down. "That's enough jingling."

"Hey, you know our deal. No sex talk." Claire made a

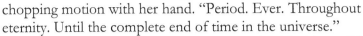

chopping motion with her hand. "Period. Ever. Throughout eternity. Until the complete end of time in the universe."

"Yes, my delicate flower child," Deborah said with a solid dose of sarcasm. Then she sighed. "It would be nice to have a girlfriend down here. Someone I could talk with openly about my life now and then. You kids don't want to hear what I have to say about much of anything these days."

There was no denying that. Ronnie, especially, had gone out of her way to avoid the sound of her mother's voice as she struggled to find sure footing in her life after leaving her own smoldering mess of a marriage.

She looked down at Katie, who was picking at the bark on the tree below. Being able to vent to her sisters had been a lifesaver. And having Grady there helped, too. Ronnie's whole body warmed just thinking about all of the therapy sessions she'd had in his bed. Hell, even Chester and Manny had lent her an ear now and then as she'd worked through her anger and frustrations. And then there was Ruby and her wonderful baked goodies that would help to sweeten Ronnie's disposition whenever ...

"Oh! I know, you could talk to Ruby," Ronnie suggested. "She's about your age, and your husbands are good buddies."

Deborah wrinkled her nose. "I don't think that's a—"

"Ruby is wonderful, Mother," Ronnie said, cutting her off. "You need to get past that whole gold digger idea you have when it comes to her. She is clearly not in this for the money."

"Veronica, this has nothing to do with my previous misdirected hostilities when it comes to Ruby."

"Then why not talk to her? She's kind and funny, and she really—"

"She is sleeping with my father. The idea of talking about marital relations with my stepmother, let alone certain ... uh ... physiological predicaments in the bedroom for those of us past menopause, makes me shudder."

Claire shuddered as well from head to toe. Talk about abnormal psychology, Ronnie thought with a smirk. Ever since Claire had walked in on their mom and Manny in bed doing the wild thing, the big baby ran from the room at the slightest show of affection between Deborah and their new stepfather.

"What kind of physiological predicaments?" Katie hollered from below. "Is this something that changes after you have a baby?"

"Partly," Deborah called back. "But more because of diminishing estrogen that comes with middle age."

Ronnie had sat through a wince-filled evening of her mother's "Tales of the Menopausal" back when they were both still sporting their first wedding bands—well, Deborah's first one. Ronnie didn't have plans to ever wear another, especially after learning how frustrating going through the physical and mental shifts coming her way at mid-life might be. Having a male around then could end with her behind bars alongside her ex before she made it through "the change" and back to solid ground.

Maybe it was a good time to change the subject and focus on the bigger black cloud sitting on the horizon. "How do you know Dad's coming solo?" Ronnie asked Claire. Katie hadn't said anything about that earlier.

"It was in the message he left with Jess."

"It doesn't matter if his girlfriend is with him or not," Deborah said.

Ronnie refocused on her mom. "What do you mean?"

"The scene will be the same as it was when you were kids and Randy arrived home from one of his business trips. You girls will fawn all over him, as if the king had returned from battle. And there I'll stand in the background, having been the one who held the castle together while he was gone, watching all the merriment and listening to the squeals of delight."

"I don't remember squealing," Claire said.

Ronnie frowned at her sister. "That's not the point."

"I know, but I'd like to have it on record that Kate was the squealer."

"You squeal, too, Claire," Katie hollered up.

"Just once," Deborah continued. "I wish that I'd been greeted that way when returning from somewhere. Then again, I was *always* home with you girls, so there was never a place to return from."

"From where to return," Katie corrected Deborah's grammar.

"Shut it, Professor Weisenheimer!" Claire yelled back.

To their mom, Ronnie said, "We were happy to see Dad, that's true. But you were our rock. No matter what, you were there day after day."

"Annoyingly so, at times," Deborah said under her breath.

Ronnie wasn't sure if that comment was aimed at them or at the situation, so she kept silent and looked out over the campground, which was about three-quarters full of RVs at the moment. It appeared that Jess's school website project showcasing the RV park was paying off already.

"I want to see Dad," Claire said, her tone serious. "I want to ask him some questions."

"Like what?" Deborah asked.

"The same thing I want to ask you—why did you wait so long to end your marriage if you were both unhappy?"

Her mom frowned down at her hands. "I wasn't always unhappy."

A scoff slipped out before Ronnie could stop it.

Deborah aimed a scowl her way. "What? I wasn't. You girls don't remember what it was like in the beginning when I was more important to your father than his career. Back when we were younger, struggling for every dollar, finding joy in the smallest things, like Veronica's first steps." To

Claire, she said, "And your adorable baby giggles."

"What about me?" Katie called up. "Or were you miserable by the time I came along?" There was a gasp from below. "Oh no, was I the reason your marriage tanked?"

"No, Kathryn," Deborah called back. "Even though you came out of the womb thinking the world revolved around you, your entry into our lives had nothing to do with our marriage going sour." She took a deep breath, shaking her head. "We did that all by ourselves."

"You were pretty unhappy by the time I was in junior high," Claire said. "I could tell."

"That's true. Your father was making good money by then, but that meant traveling a lot. I was bored. And lonely. And tired of being a single parent." She made a frowny-smile. "I'm afraid I took that misery out on you girls."

"You tried to live through us," Ronnie said. Even though that wasn't really news to anyone, looking at it through a different lens at this moment made her understand her mom's periodic obsessive behavior a little more.

"Yeah, and then your father would come home and hold a mirror in front of my face, making me see what I was becoming." Deborah groaned. "We'd have some bang-up fights then, throwing everything at each other but the kitchen sink."

Claire snorted. "I remember. I'd crank up the television volume super loud to try to drown it all out, but then I'd get in trouble for watching TV too loud and you guys would send me outside."

Ronnie remembered the fights, too. She'd usually blame her mom for starting them, wishing she'd go away on a trip for a while and leave them with their dad.

Criminy, life was messy. And then Ronnie had gone and tried to escape into a fake perfect life with a big fancy house, snobby social club gatherings, and white picket fences. Talk about living in a self-made prison.

Looking out over the dusty desert landscape with the cacti sticking up like patches of bristly porcupine quills under the big blue sky, she understood now why she'd stalled here in Jackrabbit Junction in spite of her original plans. It was hard to be fenced in out here. For years, she'd been a primped, refined stable pony. Now, she could run free.

Maybe it was time for her mom to run free, too. Maybe Deborah already was, and that was why she was struggling so much, turning to the bottle more than ever.

"Dad coming for a day doesn't change anything between the three of us and you, Mom," Ronnie said, reaching out to touch her mom's hand. Her skin was cold, but her return squeeze was strong. "You need to allow us this moment to regroup with him, though."

"I know. I know."

"If you're worried he's going to turn us against you, somehow—" Claire started.

"No, it's not that." Deborah let out a harsh laugh. "I think I've done more damage on that front over the years than he ever could with just words."

Ronnie wasn't sure what to say to that, because there was a layer of truth in it. Instead, she threw out, "We could go shopping today in Yuccaville, if you like."

"Some of us have to work, you know," Katie shouted.

"We could go shopping without Kate," Claire said loudly with a smile. "And talk about her behind her back."

Katie aimed two middle fingers in their direction.

"Actually, I can't." Deborah let go of Ronnie's hand and brushed some dust off her slacks. "Manuel wants to go to Tucson today to do some last-minute Christmas shopping. He loves to see the stores all decorated for the holiday, and I promised to go with him." She chuckled. "He's like a little boy when it comes to Christmas. Takes me back to when you girls were young, and I'd go all out to decorate the house and the yard, trying to keep Santa real as long as I could."

"You really were obsessive about decorating," Claire said, her smile and wink taking any sting out of her words. "But it made for a fun holiday. Although I hated those damned Christmas dresses you'd always make us wear."

"But you were so cute!" Deborah pinched her cheek. "Like three adorable dolls, your hair in ringlets and all."

Claire rolled her eyes and faked a gag.

Katie's head popped over the top of the roof's edge, the ladder framing her pink cheeks. "Remember the year Claire rolled in the mud with her dress right before we were supposed to go to Gramps' and Grandma's? Boy howdy, did she get in trouble that day." Katie's grin was double wide.

"Kathryn Lynette, get down off that ladder right now!" Deborah popped to her feet, stepping carefully toward her youngest daughter.

Katie's chin jutted. "Not until you get down here with me. I want to be included in this Hallmark moment."

"There is no Hallmark moment," Claire said. "We're more like those monkeys in *The Jungle Book* fighting over bananas." She followed their mom. "Now get down before you fall down, like Gramps did."

Katie pointed at Claire. "If memory serves me right, Gramps didn't fall, you and Henry were horsing around and knocked the ladder over."

"Shut up and get down, coo-coo-ca-chu."

Katie's cheeks darkened. "I'm going to—"

"Kathryn!" Deborah stepped between her two daughters, same as she had many, many times before. "Get down right now so that I can come down there and pinch your arm good and hard for risking my grandchild's life up here."

"Fine!" Katie narrowed her gaze. "But when you retell this story someday, be sure to mention that I'm the one who got you down off the dang roof." She cast a glare at Claire and then Ronnie. "And don't the rest of you—with your tiny, mean hearts and green furry fingers—forget that."

Claire chuckled, turning to Ronnie. "Are you coming or what, Grinchy?"

"Sure thing." Ronnie stood. "We don't want all of the Whos down in Whoville to cry boo-hoo now, do we?"

Chapter Nine:
It's Beginning to Look a Lot Like Christmas
OH, CRAP!

Monday, December 24th
Christmas Eve at The Shaft

R andy Morgan was shorter than Mac had expected. Maybe it was because of all the stories he'd heard about Randy since meeting Claire, who looked up to her father like he was bigger than life.

Or maybe it had to do with Deborah and the tall tales she'd told about her evil ex-husband, including the one about Randy having an affair. At least that was the unexpected news Claire had told Mac when she'd stopped by his barstool to grab another beer for her father and the order of fries she'd put in earlier.

Judging from Claire's big smile, this change in the story of the downfall of their parents' marriage was a happy surprise. With a promise to fill him in more later, she'd returned to the table in the far corner where she and her sisters and her father were enjoying a family meal for the first time in almost a year. Mac had opted to join them later, after they'd had some time to catch up.

Besides, he needed some time to build up to showing

Claire the ring and popping a very big, tall, intimidating, nerve-wracking question. The King Kong of all questions. At least that's what it felt like.

"I need two more pale ale taps," Butch said to Gary, the bartender, and then took a seat on the barstool next to Mac.

With Kate and Claire offline, Butch was playing waiter to the handful of patrons hanging around this afternoon. He planned on closing early today so that the Morgan family Christmas Eve festivities could go on into the night without a crowd there to interfere. Mac was breathing easier knowing there'd be fewer people there when he finally buckled down and pulled that ring box out of his pocket.

"When's Grady supposed to be here?" he asked Butch as he watched Bill Murray relive glimpses of his past in the movie *Scrooged*, which was playing on the flatscreen high up behind the bar. The television was muted, but Mac had seen the movie often enough to hear the actors' lines in his head.

"Any time now." Butch stared up at the flat screen, too, fidgeting with a bar napkin. "When I was delivering some drinks over by the jukebox," he said in a low voice, "I heard Claire ask her dad about having had an affair."

Mac nodded, glancing toward Butch, stirring his virgin version of a Tom Collins. He wanted to keep his head clear tonight, so he was avoiding alcohol altogether. Meeting his potential future father-in-law had his palms sweating throughout the morning. He'd blown it with Deborah without even trying. He needed at least one of Claire's parents to not want to throw darts at him on a daily basis.

"Yeah, she just stopped by to get a refill and told me that there was no affair."

"Really? So Deborah was making that up?"

Mac shrugged. "I don't know the details yet."

Gary slid the two drinks across the bar. "Hey Butch, how do you feel about me taking some time off over the holiday? My mom hasn't been feeling good lately. I might need to call in once or twice to go over and take care of her."

"Yeah, sure," Butch said, smiling a little too wide.

"Thanks. Sorry to leave you short-handed while you're visiting your family, but I don't know if Mom will make it another Christmas."

"Don't even worry about this place. Family is far more important."

After Gary walked away, Mac turned to Butch. "You know, I used to bartend back in college now and then. If you need some help behind the bar, I can fill in."

"Thanks, man. I might take you up on that when Kate and I are back home visiting." He frowned toward the corner table. "Although I'm getting the feeling that I'm the only one who will be going home this Christmas."

"What do you mean?"

"Kate's avoiding me whenever I bring up taking her to meet my family. I think she's building up the nerve to tell me she doesn't want to go."

"Is that going to be a problem?"

He shrugged and stood. "Not yet, but you know that old proverb—'If the mountain won't come to Muhammad.' " Butch grabbed the beers. "I want my parents to meet the woman I love before our kid is born. One way or another, I'll make it happen."

Mac sipped his lemony drink as Butch walked away. Then his gaze slid to the corner table. Ronnie was opening a small present as the rest of them watched.

What was it with these Morgan girls and their inability to commit to anything? Was it a result of their parents' turbulent marriage? Or did it stem from something else? A genetic disposition to be non-monogamous? They were mammals after all, where monogamy was only a 10 percent occurrence, unlike 90 percent of the bird species out there, so with numbers like those, commitment phobia probably wasn't really …

Bah humbug! Where was he going with this?

Mac returned to the movie, letting Bill Murray take away his troubles. Frank Cross had just painfully met the Ghost of Christmas Present when someone bumped his elbow.

"Hey, Mac," Ronnie said. "Any word when Grady will be here?"

"Butch said any time now."

"Good. Dad is looking forward to meeting him." Ronnie chewed on her lower lip as she frowned at the door.

"Don't worry," Mac told her. "Everyone likes the sheriff of Cholla County. Your dad probably will, too. If not, Grady can throw him in jail until he comes around."

She smirked. "Not everyone likes him. My mother is the president of the Anti-Sheriff Fan Club."

"Okay, so everyone but your mother." Mac chuckled without humor. "Deborah takes great joy in torturing any man who dares to come too close to her daughters."

"Yeah, she does," Ronnie said with a small smile. "Maybe that's not such a bad thing after all."

"What?! As one of the poor guys suffering from her daily abuse, I strongly disagree."

Ronnie laughed. "Well, if it's any relief, I don't think Dad is into reenacting the Spanish Inquisition with you." She paused to order a lemon-lime soda from Gary. Back to Mac, she added, "He told Claire that you're a pretty low risk based on you owning your house, having a diversified stock portfolio, and holding steady for a bunch of years at your job. Very stable."

Jesus, that made him sound dull as hell. And how did Randy know about his stock portfolio? Claire must have mentioned it. Was that how she saw him? Steady? Low risk? Snoresville? Who would want to spend their life with such a person? Day after day, the same old story?

One of the reasons he'd been drawn to Claire was her spark. Her propensity to get into trouble had brought color to his black-and-white world.

"Great," Mac said without feeling it.

Ronnie clapped him on the shoulder. "No, that's a good thing in Dad-speak. He doesn't like high-risk ventures."

Then being married to Deborah must have had him pulling his hair out. She screamed high-risk from her sharp pink claws to her fake alligator-skin boots.

"When Grady shows up, will you ask him to wait here with you? I want to introduce him to Dad myself. Maybe try to smooth the way."

Smooth the way? "Why? What does your dad know about Grady that could cause bumps?"

Her forehead lined. "Well, being that Grady is a lawman, he's a high risk. Beyond the potential to get shot on the job, Dad is concerned about the trouble Grady's work could bring back to me."

"Back to *you*? The Queen of Hitman Central?" Mac let out a hard, sharp laugh. "That's rich."

Ronnie punched him in the shoulder. "Shhhh." She aimed a quick frown toward the corner.

"Hold up. You haven't told your dad about the whole mess with your ex yet, have you?"

She shook her head. "I told him we're divorced. That's all he needs to know for now."

"He's your father, Ronnie."

"Trust me, he does not need to worry about this, too. He has enough stress with his job as it is. So mum's the word or I'll key your pickup."

Mac did a double-take. Damn, these Morgan sisters played dirty when push came to shove. "Fine, my lips are sealed. So, keep your key in your pocket, or I'll report you to the county sheriff for vandalism. He's a hardass, I hear."

She giggled. "Oh, he can be." She held out her hand. "Deal?"

Frowning, he shook her hand. "Sure, but I really think

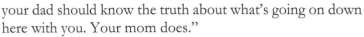

your dad should know the truth about what's going on down here with you. Your mom does."

"Yeah, but she's weathered this kind of craziness with us most of her life."

"True. And the insanity *does* appear to be hereditary."

Ronnie pinched his arm. "You're a funny boy, Mac. Be good to me, though, or I'll turn you into a high risk, too. It's my special power."

Gary handed Ronnie her drink, and after a hip-bump into Mac's side, she returned to the corner table.

"You want another one of those?" Gary asked, pointing at Mac's drink.

"Please," Mac said, with a nod.

"You want some lead in this one?"

"Not yet."

As Gary went about making and delivering another virgin Tom Collins, Mac returned to *Scrooged*. Bill was in an elevator with a fake Grim Reaper. Mac could relate. After that assessment from Claire's dad, he was feeling pretty dead in the water himself when it came to that engagement ring.

Stable.

Ugh. When had he gone and turned into one of the walls he designed and built for a living?

Frank Cross was wrapping things up and encouraging the viewers to sing along with him on the TV when a deep voice said, "Is this seat taken by your invisible girlfriend?"

Mac grinned, turning to Grady Harrison, who was not in his sheriff getup at the moment. In fact, he looked freshly shaven and wrinkle-free, and his black wavy hair was still damp on the ends.

"Nope," Mac said. "I was saving it for another poor sucker who might be dreading having to meet the new stranger in town."

"Oh, Christ. I thought I was a decade past this meet-the-parents song and dance," Grady said, taking a seat before casting a glance around the bar. "I'm sweating like I'm back in high school on prom night with a boxed corsage in hand."

"All four of them are in the far corner," Mac told him.

Grady stilled for a moment, then made a low grunting sound in his throat and turned back toward the bar. "Why did I think he'd have blond hair and narrower shoulders?"

"I thought he'd be about your height," Mac said. "Not shorter than me."

"You're no shrimp. What are you? Six-two and one-eighty-five?"

"Just about and a few pounds more." Mac took a sip from his glass. "You're good at that guessing game. If you ever lose your job as sheriff, you could work at the circus."

Grady chuckled, and then ordered a lager from Gary.

"What's that?" he asked, pointing at Mac's drink.

"Tom Collins minus the alcohol."

"Toeing the line tonight, huh?"

Mac nodded. "I don't need any help stepping on my tongue."

"Yeah." Grady took the beer Gary held out for him and nodded his thanks. After he took a sip, he said, "I need to take the edge off for this. I tried playing things the cold sober way with Deborah." He sighed. "That shit went south faster than a speeding bullet. That woman's tongue is twice-forked, I swear."

Chuckling, Mac raised his glass in a mock toast. "If it's any consolation, Ronnie stopped by a bit ago and told me that she plans to introduce you personally, hoping to help smooth the way."

Grady slowly looked Mac's way, his gaze tightening. "Why would she need to do that?"

"Uhhh." Shit. He probably shouldn't have said anything and just kept drinking while watching the movie credits. "To help you out."

Grady set his drink down. "Why do I need smoothing

already?"

Of course Grady would sniff out the truth. He hadn't made his way up the career ladder to county sheriff by being a Barney Fife. Although Barney certainly kept things entertaining.

"No reason."

"I can tell you're lying."

Mac frowned. "How?"

"Never mind. Why does Veronica need to smooth the way for me already?"

Mac sighed. "Because apparently you're a high risk for her."

A smile spread across Grady's face, draping from ear to ear. He laughed, low and loud. A belly laugh.

"I know," Mac said, grinning as well. "That was my reaction, too."

"I'm the one who's high risk. Oh, that's rich."

"Yeah." Mac cast a glance toward the corner, catching Ronnie's frown as she stared in their direction. He turned his back to her, focusing forward again. "She hasn't told her dad about Lyle's mess."

Grady sobered. "You're kidding."

"Nope."

"None of it?"

"Only that they are divorced."

"So, when Randy finds out and learns that I knew about it and didn't tell him, I'm going to be stuck between a rock and a hard place."

"Yeah, but you're the sheriff. Rocks and hard places are your bread and butter."

Grady sent him a sideways squint as he took a swallow from his beer.

"Hey, you being high risk is better than what I am."

One of Grady's eyebrows cocked. "A geotechnician?"

"Stable and dull."

"Based on what?"

"My numbers on paper."

"Well, judging by the number and length of the reports I've written up since Claire and *you* came to Jackrabbit Junction, I'd peg you as a very high risk. How many times have you been almost killed now?"

Mac stirred his drink. "About one less time than Claire."

Grady harumphed. "There you have it. And where's Butch fall on the risk scale?"

"I don't know yet, but I'll bet a ten-spot that a glance at his risk graph is far more exciting than my steady and stable line."

Holding his glass of beer toward Mac, Grady said, "Here's to burning those risk graphs."

After they clinked glasses, Mac glanced toward the corner table again.

"Looks like we're about to have some company."

Claire and Kate were heading their way, while Ronnie stayed back at the table still talking to their dad.

"Hello, boys," Claire said, as she joined them at the bar.

"Claire." Grady nodded and then leaned back to peer around her, where Kate was partially hiding from the sheriff. Mac wondered what she'd done now to make her shy away from the law.

"What are you doing back there, trouble?" Grady asked.

Kate stepped into view, her gaze challenging. "I'm innocent, Sheriff."

"Right." He laughed again, almost as loud as before.

She thumbed behind her. "But my dad's here, and he wants to talk to you about the legalities of getting free milk from a cow before actually attempting to make a purchase."

Grady's face tightened in a wince.

"Ronnie sent us to get you, Grady," Claire said. "And she told us to stay away so Dad could have a moment with you." She leaned into Mac, draping her arm over his shoulder.

"They're waiting for you at the table."

"Damn." Grady sighed. "Here we go again." He grabbed his beer, aiming a wrinkled brow at Mac. "Keep your fingers crossed this one goes better than the last."

Mac held up his crossed fingers. "We'll be cheering you on from here."

Kate took Grady's stool after he walked away, smiling after him like she was sending the evil overlord off to be torn into pieces by wild dogs. "I wish I could be one of those tiny Who things that live on a speck of dust, so I could float up to Sheriff Grinch's hideout and eavesdrop as Dad chews on him for screwing around with my sister."

A whispered curse came from Claire. "Okay, first of all, you're mixing *Horton Hears a Who* with *How the Grinch Stole Christmas.*"

"I don't care."

"Second, Dad is not going to chew on Grady. He's just going to ask about his job and get to know him better."

Mac looked up at Claire. "How come Butch and I didn't have to do the solo meet-and-greet deal with your dad?"

"Because Kate and I have been talking about you guys for months over the phone to him. Dad already knows a ton about you two. But Ronnie hadn't said a peep about Grady until she knew Dad was coming south. So he has a doubly good reason to be suspicious about Grady."

"Poor sucker," Mac said, shaking his head.

"Ha!" Kate bristled. "It's good for Mr. Big and Tough Sheriff to get a taste of his own medicine."

"Kate," Claire said, scowling at her sister. "You really need to work on taming that mad monkey in your head. Its tendency to throw bananas at people is disturbing."

"Shut up, Claire." Kate growled at her, but then did an about-face and sported an overly shiny smile as Butch joined them.

"What's the story with the three birdies over there in the

corner?" he asked.

"Dad's grilling Grady," Claire explained.

Butch cringed. "Oh, boy. Grady's going to need a few more beers before the night is over."

Rubbing her hands together, Kate grinned. "I hope so. That'll be payback for the last time he had me locked up in his jail cell."

"Dear Lord, you nutcracker." Claire reached out and flicked Kate in the forehead. "Go back in your cage until you can act civil out amongst the humans."

Kate bared her teeth at Claire. "Keep calling me names like that and I'll bite you, I swear."

"So, what's the story with your dad not really having an affair?" Butch asked, wrapping his arms around Kate from behind.

Mac wasn't sure if Butch was showing affection with that move or just corralling Kate. Probably both.

"There was nothing actually physical going on between him and the other woman." Claire reached for Mac's glass. "There was some flirting, but nothing happened until he was separated from Mom."

"Mom read one of the emails the lady had sent to him," Kate continued the story. "And she automatically assumed there was a full-on affair in progress. Dad tried to deny it at first, but then he realized that this was the catalyst they needed to put an end to their years of misery together. It was the one thing that would make Mom agree to a divorce, so he went along with it."

"Even at the risk of tarnishing his reputation?" Butch asked.

"Yep," Claire said. "He assessed the situation and decided it was worth the negative exposure to be free."

"Although," Kate countered with a frown, "I don't know if he took into account how hard it would hit Mom."

"True. But she has Manny now, who adores her." Claire

sipped Mac's drink. "Yum, this is good. A little sweet and a little tart, sparkly."

"I know." Mac patted her backside. "Sort of reminds me of you."

She pulled him closer, kissing him on the temple. "My dad is looking forward to learning more about what you do back in Tucson."

Oh, sure. The boring work he did while living his mundane life. He tried to hide his tension about being low risk behind a smile. It was no wonder Claire didn't like staying in Tucson with him for more than a couple of nights. The dusty pitstop of Jackrabbit Junction offered way more excitement in one afternoon than he could in a month.

But still, maybe she was just what he needed. Maybe if she would marry him, that would give him the impetus to change things up and add more hiccups to his routine. Hell, he might eventually throw his routine out the window entirely.

"Speaking of eager parents," Butch said, spinning Kate's barstool so that she faced him. "We need to talk about the trip to see my family."

"Valentine." Kate sighed, looking down at her hands. "I don't want to go."

Butch shared a knowing look with Mac before returning his focus to Kate. "I figured that when you buried your luggage in the back of the closet this morning."

Her gaze returned to his. "You noticed that, huh?"

He nodded. "I have another idea."

"What?"

"How about instead of going to see my family for Christmas, we fly to Vegas."

Her head tipped to the side slightly. "Why would we fly to Las Vegas? Is there another antique car show going on?"

"No, silly. To get married."

Seriously?!!! Mac's jaw gaped. Had Butch really popped the question that Mac had been agonizing over for days? Just like that? No bended knee? No rambling beginning? No ring in sight? A straight-up blurt, "Hey, let's get married."

Mac turned to Claire. Her wide eyes mirrored his surprise. She seemed to be holding her breath, too, waiting along with Butch for Kate's response.

"Married?" Kate asked in an outrageous tone, as if he'd suggested riding in a hot air balloon clear to the moon.

"Yes, Kate. Married."

"To you?"

Butch's grin wavered. "Of course to me, crazy."

Claire winced, leaning in to whisper to Mac. "She doesn't like that word."

"Did you just call me the C-word?" Kate asked. Two bright pink spots lit on her cheeks.

Butch held up his hands in surrender. "I'm sorry, sweetheart. That was a slip of the tongue."

"Yeah." Kate snorted extra loud. "Your tongue seems to be slipping and sliding all over the place. A reindeer on ice has better footing than you right now."

"How about it?" Butch pushed, back to grinning. "Do you want to get married with the King of Rock and Roll officiating?"

She crossed her arms. "No."

"No to the King or to me?"

"Both."

"Why not?" Claire butted in, and then covered her mouth and muttered "Sorry," behind her hand.

Kate sputtered for a breath or two, and then scowled at Claire and Butch in turn. "Because."

"Give me a better reason than that, baby," Butch said, his arms crossed now, too.

Kate's chin lifted. "Fine. I don't like the way you squeeze the toothpaste tube."

A caw-like, gobbling sound came from Claire, who then

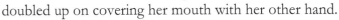

doubled up on covering her mouth with her other hand.

"For another," Kate continued. "I'm not ready yet."

Hey, that was Claire's line. At least it was one of the explanations Mac had expected to hear after she'd rejected his proposal.

Butch's gaze tightened into a hard squint. "Fine, but don't think I'm giving up that easily, bad mama jama."

She grabbed him by the front of his shirt and pulled him closer. "You better not, or I'll hunt you down and make you beg for mercy."

He growled in his throat. "I do like it when I get roughed up and tumbled."

"What is this sick and twisted dance you two are doing?" Claire asked, once again on the same wavelength as Mac.

"It's called love, fruitcake," Kate said and then planted a very wet kiss on Butch's mouth.

"They're weird," Claire said to Mac as the kiss continued.

He scratched his head. "I'm confused by what just happened here. So, your sister won't marry Butch, *and* she's not going with him to see his family, but that's okay with him?"

"I think that about nails it."

Kate put some breathing room between Butch's and her lips. Her fingernails trailed down his shirt. "I'll call you once a day when you're gone and let you know how things are going here at the bar."

He caught her hand and kissed her open palm. "Make it twice. Or I'll get lonely and probably die from a broken heart."

Kate started to lean toward him again, but Claire stuck her hand between their faces.

"Okay, Romeo and Juliet. I hate to break up this 'cuckoo for Cocoa Puffs' moment, but Ronnie is waving us over." Claire grabbed Kate's arm and tugged her to her feet. "Let's go."

After a wink at Mac, Claire led her sister back to where Grady and Ronnie sat with Randy.

Butch dropped onto the barstool, a bit moony-eyed as he grinned at Mac. "That's the fourth time this month that she's rejected me."

Mac did a double-take. "You've asked her to marry you *four* times?"

"More than that." He waved off the number as if proposing to Kate was part of his weekly routine, along with taking the trash to the curb. "Last week she rejected me because she doesn't like the way I fold towels. The week before that, it was how I stack the dirty dishes in the dishwasher."

Mac shook his head in disbelief. "Yet you keep trying."

"Sure." Butch shrugged. "One of these times, she'll run out of excuses, and then that girl is mine."

Over by the pool tables, a guy in a red and white cowboy hat with mistletoe pinned to the front of it held up an empty beer pitcher. "Hey, Butch. Another pitcher back here."

"Duty calls," Butch said. "And Gary's on break." He slipped behind the bar and began filling a pitcher with beer.

Mac's attention returned to the television where he recognized the beginning scenes of *Home Alone*. How fitting. That was his life story these days. Home alone in Tucson. He puffed his cheeks, slowly letting out a pent-up breath.

Well, crap. He leaned his elbows on the bar, his gut churning more than ever about popping the question to Claire after watching Butch crash and burn.

Maybe he should hide the ring away for now and focus on something less worrisome.

Or maybe he should take a page from Butch's book.

"If the mountain will not come to Muhammad," Mac said under his breath as he stirred his drink, "then Muhammad must go to the mountain."

Yeah, maybe that was the trick.

Chapter Ten:

Jingle Bells
Balls

Tuesday, December 25th
Christmas Day

R onnie spilled the beans.
Literally.
As in the red plastic cereal bowl full of chili beans that someone had left teetering on the edge of a shelf in the refrigerator. All it had taken was one tiny nudge as she reached for some eggnog-flavored coffee creamer and down they went, splattering beans here, there, and everywhere … including on the toes of her new leather boots.

"Smelly buggers!" she muttered and rushed to the cupboard under the kitchen sink to grab an old rag from the stack Ruby kept there.

Damned Chester. He was the king of beans, often eating them straight from the can for breakfast. She was going to give him a good pinch when she returned to Ruby's rec room, where most everyone was hanging out amidst the crumpled wrapping paper and discarded boxes, including Grady. He and his aunt Millie had shown up in time for Manny's holiday brunch starring prickly pear pancakes and southwest-style frittatas.

Dragging the trash can over, she began mopping up the bean mess, starting with her boots, before Grady came into the kitchen and saw the mess she'd made on the toes of his gorgeous Christmas gift.

She'd certainly made enough of a mess for him to clean up otherwise, what with the hitmen, the FBI, and that damned diamond killer, who seemed to be inching closer by the day. Then Ronnie had gone and added her father to the list of reasons why Grady should probably run away from her and not look back.

Scratching her cheek with the back of her wrist, she sniffed and picked up a hint of garlic. Or was that onion powder? She held the rag up to her nose, grimacing. Maybe both. Yep, definitely Chester's beans.

She walked to the sink and rinsed the cloth, frowning out through the kitchen window at nothing in particular while her thoughts drifted back to The Shaft with her dad and Grady at the corner table.

High risk, her dad had called the sheriff of Cholla County. She wrung out the rag. It was true, only not in the way her father meant. Grady was a high risk to her heart, because the silly organ hadn't seemed to learn any lessons after the beating it took over the last five years with Lyle.

Although, looking back, her heart had only been phoning it in most days, so it was more her ego that had taken a bruising and been left whimpering in the gutter. This time, if she didn't take care, her heart wouldn't escape so easily, and no amount of gin and tonic would numb that pain. Her mother's ongoing love affair with cognac was proof of that.

Grady ... He'd been tense from the moment he sat down next to her at The Shaft, his knee bouncing—sometimes bumping hers—as her dad hit the poor guy with one question after another, starting with his history, then onto his life as a badge-toting lawman, and ending with whether he planned to have a family eventually.

At the mention of "family," Ronnie had wanted to crawl under the table. Better yet, run out of the bar and keep sprinting down the road. Forever. Hell, she and Grady were barely past the slightly awkward dating stage. Her dad was jumping way too far into the future with the whole *family* idea. Especially with the black cloud Ronnie had to live under, thanks to her piece-of-shit ex.

She had opened her mouth at that point to tell her father that very thing, only gingerly since Grady was sitting right next to her. But then Grady had taken her hand in his and gallantly informed her dad that he intended to do everything he could to keep anyone from hurting his daughter.

She'd made the dumb mistake of looking into Grady's eyes then. What she saw staring back from the amber depths made her heart clang in her ears. Her father was wrong. High risk? No, Grady was an *extreme* risk. A threat far greater than any creepy Grinches that might come looking for her.

In that moment with her hand warm from Grady's touch, the sounds of The Shaft and her father's voice had faded away. There had only been Grady and this unappeasable, constant need to be with him no matter what.

No matter that she was this year's cover girl for *Hitman Magazine*.

No matter that she might never be out from under her ex's long and deadly shadow.

No matter that she didn't have a suitable family history to live in the public eye, let alone a proper wardrobe, to be a sheriff's wife.

She'd wanted to hold onto his hand forever, come what may. But Jackrabbit Junction was no Mayberry, and Ronnie also needed to remember her place—which would probably be best for Grady and her family if it were in a dusty *pueblo* somewhere far south of the Mexican border.

She wrung out the rag once more and returned to her current mess. From now on she probably should focus on cleaning up one bowl of spilled beans at a time.

A couple of minutes later, she was trying to reach the last few beans that had fallen behind the deli drawers in the refrigerator when Katie waltzed into the kitchen.

"Hey," Katie said, tossing her empty can of ginger ale in the recycle bin. "Why are you cleaning the fridge right now? It's still Christmas in the rec room, you know, and your boyfriend is getting another dressing down from *your* mother."

"For what now?"

"I didn't hang around long enough to hear that part, but it's probably something to do with breathing oxygen while being a sheriff and screwing around with her oldest child." Katie reached over Ronnie's head to grab another can of ginger ale off the refrigerator shelf. "So, what's with playing Holly Homemaker here in the kitchen? Are you avoiding a particular law dog, same as I am?"

Ronnie rolled her eyes. Katie really needed to get over this cop allergy of hers. "I spilled the beans."

"Really? What did Grady say?"

Looking up from where she was kneeling on the floor, Ronnie asked, "About what?"

"You being in love with him." Katie pointed downward. "It was the boots, wasn't it? They are gorgeous. I might have even told Grady I loved him if he'd given me those babies."

"Shhhh!" Ronnie shot a glance toward the doorway. "First of all, I'm not in love," she whispered. "This thing with Grady is just one big sticky popcorn ball of lust."

"Fine, if you say so, but you don't have to scowl and flare your nostrils at me about it, Ebenezer Scrooge." Katie leaned against the counter, a smartass grin rounding her cheeks. "So then you told Grady about your little trick up top, right?"

Ronnie sat back on her heels, the last of the wayward beans in her hand. "What trick up top?"

"You know," Katie said, cupping her hands in front of her chest. "The boob job you had a few years back."

"What in the planets are you talking about?"

Katie snickered, sounding remarkably like Chester. "I'm just messing with you. I know you stuff your bra and that those saggy ol' jingle balls of yours are the real deal."

"Saggy!" Ronnie threw a bean at her sister, who giggled as she dodged it. "I meant I spilled an actual bowl of chili beans, you no-good bang gunk stinkin' crisp."

Katie laughed, holding onto the small belly bump now showing under her pink velvet tunic. "Nice swearing. I see Claire got you to watch *A Christmas Story* again."

"Actually, Grady and I watched it last night after he drove me home from The Shaft."

"Home?"

"*His* home." Ronnie's place was still here at the RV park, both physically and mentally. Pretending to play house with Grady was a slippery slope.

"So, he made it through Dad's interrogation and still wanted to sleep next to you." She whistled low. "You really have that boy wrapped around your finger."

Returning to the sink to rinse the rag again, she frowned at her sister. "I'm afraid it might be the other way around."

"Well, no duh."

Ronnie shrugged off her smartass sister. "Enough about me, tell me about Mom."

Claire walked backward through the kitchen doorway, hollering toward the rec room, "If you'd stop touching it for a minute, Chester, the thing would stop popping up!" She turned around, the empty tortilla chip bowl in her hand. "Oh, hey, what are you two misfit toys doing off your island?"

"Ronnie spilled the beans," Katie said.

"I thought *you* were going to tell Mom about the whole-not-really-an-affair deal, since you're her favorite."

"I'm not her favorite, Ronnie is." Katie crossed her arms. "And why do I have to be the one to break the news? You two were the ones who climbed up on the roof with her. You're like the three *amigos* now."

Claire dropped the empty chip bowl on the table. "Did you tell her or not, Little Cindy-Lou Who?"

"You and Butch need to zip it with that nickname." Katie reached up and yanked the red bow out of her hair. "Just because I decided to wear a ribbon in my hair on Christmas, you two have to poke fun at me."

Chuckling, Ronnie rinsed the rag in the sink. "Katie, you do kind of look like Cindy-Lou. At least the illustration from the actual Dr. Seuss book."

"Whatever." She messed up her hair, leaving horns sticking up here and there. "Now who do I look like?"

"A rabid pregnant zombie," Claire said, and then ducked when Katie scooped up some of the few remaining beans from the red bowl and whipped them at her.

When the beans stopped flying, Claire asked, "So, did you tell Mom or not?"

Katie nodded. "At first she didn't believe me, but after she stopped fighting the truth, she sort of melted onto the bed." She made a frowny face. "Then the tears started."

"That's not surprising," Ronnie said. "She's probably going to go through another round of the stages of grief."

"Let's just hope she turns to Manny this time instead of the cognac bottle."

Katie scratched at something on the counter. "I tried to tell her that this was for the best, because they had both been unhappy for so long in their marriage, but I don't know if she's at a place yet where she can accept that."

Claire opened a new bag of tortilla chips and dumped them into the bowl. "Did you mention anything about Dad's idea of possibly coming south, too?"

"No way. I wasn't going to touch that, not even with a 39-and-a-half foot pole."

Claire pointed at her. "Bonus points for using a Grinch quote."

Smiling big and opening her eyes extra wide, Katie touched her dimples and said in a Cindy-Lou voice, "Santy Claus, why are you taking our Christmas tree?"

"That's kind of creepy, Katie." Ronnie draped the rag over the faucet to dry.

"I'm not Katie," she continued. "I'm Little Cindy-Lou Who."

Chuckling, Claire said, "I double-dog dare you to use that voice on Butch in the middle of sex."

Blinking with her wide eyes, Katie continued in the creepy voice, "Oh, Valentine! I'm all toasty inside."

Claire laughed harder. "Nice, but that's the Grinch's line."

"Whatever," she said, returning to her normal voice. "Butch is going to rue all of those half-assed marriage proposals he keeps throwing at me."

Ronnie did a double-take. "What proposals?"

Katie huffed. "He keeps asking me to marry him at the craziest times. Yesterday, he proposed we elope to Las Vegas out of the blue right in front of Claire and Mac. And last week, I was ass-deep in the washer digging out dishtowels stuck to the bottom after the spin cycle when he suggests we go on a cruise and get married in international waters." She raised her hands. "Now I ask you, why on earth would a woman whose head has been over a toilet bowl for months thanks to morning sickness want to go on a cruise?"

Her jaw still gaping, Ronnie said, "But he wants to marry you, Katie."

She rolled her eyes. "I'm not marrying that man until he asks me the right way."

Chomping on a chip, Claire's brow lined. "What is the right way?"

Katie shrugged. "I'll know when it happens."

"But what if he stops asking you?" Ronnie asked.

"Then I'll ask *him*. But not when he's out behind The Shaft dry-heaving after dumping the grill's stinky grease trap."

Claire pretended to gag. "That's such a vile smell."

"He asked you right then?" Ronnie shook her head. What in the heck had prompted Butch to propose at that moment? Or any of the oddball moments he was choosing.

"Yeah, that was the first time. He might have been joking around then, or maybe getting a feel for my temperature on the subject of matrimony, but a girl likes to consider a marriage proposal without a cloud of black flies buzzing around her head in a place that doesn't reek like a hog rendering plant."

Ronnie rubbed the back of her neck. "I guess he could be showing that he loves you, no matter what."

Katie scoffed. "Or maybe he hit his head on the underside of a car hood one too many times lately."

"Well," Claire said, popping another chip in her mouth. "Keep in mind that Dad proposed to Mom in a classy restaurant and paid to have a violinist on hand playing in the background. That was very romantic and look how that turned out."

Ronnie shook her head. "You really believe that Dad wasn't actually having an affair?"

"A physical affair, no." Claire rolled the top of the bag of chips closed. "Mentally? He was probably enjoying the flirting game more than he should have been since he had a wife at home."

"And kids," Katie added.

"You and I were well out of high school by that time," Claire said, clipping the chip bag closed. "I don't feel like that's the same thing as if he'd been screwing around while we were young."

Ronnie nodded, running along the same tracks as Claire. "It doesn't matter now. The divorce is over, and he's seeing someone totally new."

"Did you give him that gift to take back to his new girlfriend before he left?" Claire asked Katie.

"Yeah. He said he'll call soon and is looking forward to returning to the desert for a longer stay. Those western South Dakota winters are brutal."

Ronnie groaned at the possible ripple effects if he actually stayed down here close to Jackrabbit Junction. "I'd like to see more of Dad, but having him and Mom within the same fifty-mile radius makes me sweaty."

"You're sweaty over everything these days," Katie said, opening the refrigerator door. "Hey, it looks more roomy in here now that you cleaned."

Claire moved behind Katie, checking it out. "Why were you cleaning the fridge, Ronnie? You left Grady out there getting gnawed on by Mom."

"Where's his aunt Millie?" Katie asked, frowning back toward the rec room. "Someone needs to keep an eye on that bruiser."

"Relax, Katie. Millie promised to be good today and not beat you up in the bathroom again."

"She didn't beat me up," Katie said, grumbling something about bullies under her breath. The left side of her face twitched visibly as she returned to the counter and opened her can of ginger ale.

Ronnie turned to Claire. "Like Katie said, I spilled the beans."

"What beans?"

"Hey, what are you three troublemakers doing in here?" Gramps asked, joining them in the kitchen in his red jeans and matching western shirt. He'd worn red on Christmas Day for as long as Ronnie could remember. "Your new stepfather wants to take a family photo with the three of you and your mom."

Groans spread around the room.

"Come on, you bunch of Scrooges," Gramps said. "At least your mom isn't making you girls wear those frilly dresses this year." He chuckled. "Claire would always manage to somehow get hers dirty before we even opened presents."

"Stupid holiday dresses," Claire said through a mouthful of chips, carrying the bowl out of the room. "Hey, Manny," Ronnie heard her yell. "I want to be in the back row."

Katie raced after Claire. "No way. I'm taller than you, and I want to hide my baby belly."

"Claire's belly is going to be bigger than yours," Deborah's voice came through the doorway loud and clear. "Especially if she doesn't quit eating all of the chips. Give those here."

"Keep it up, Mom," Claire shot back, "and I'm going to cram that coal you put in my stocking down your Christmas piehole."

Ronnie shared a grin with her grandfather. "Some things never change. Not even two thousand miles from home."

Gramps put his arm around her shoulders and gave her a kiss on the temple. He smelled like Aunt Millie's gingerbread cookies, which wasn't a surprise since he kept sneaking them off the treats table.

"I'm glad you're all down here with me," he said. "It wouldn't be Christmas without you girls." His smile wilted slightly as he stepped away from her. "I just hope your mom can stop drinking and start living again now that the big ol' jackass is gone."

She planted her hands on her hips. "By 'jackass,' you mean my father?"

"Well, if the Santa boot fits." He winked.

Ronnie puffed her cheeks and blew out a sigh, casting a worried glance toward the doorway. "I guess I'd better go rescue Grady from Mom's sharp claws."

"Probably." Gramps opened the refrigerator door. "Hey! Where's my bowl of beans?"

The End ... For Now

NOT QUITE YET!

Later that night …

Claire slipped out the screen door, stepping onto the front porch of the General Store. The porch lights were off, but thanks to the colorful glow of the Christmas lights draped along the railing, she could easily see Mac where he sat on the top porch step.

"Hey there, handsome," she said, dropping down on the step next to him. "Is your name Jingle Bells, because you sure look like you go *all* the way."

He chuckled, wrapping his arm around her middle and pulling her closer. "I go all the way and then some, baby."

She rested her head against his shoulder, snuggling into his warmth. He smelled spicy and desert fresh, the same as always, but with a touch of sugar, which was probably thanks to his aunt's sugar and spice cookies—his favorite since childhood, she'd learned tonight. After gobbling down three herself, she understood what all of the fanfare was about, too.

"What are we doing out here, McStudly? Watching for Santa to come back and drop off a forgotten present?"

"I thought I'd grab a breath of fresh air and enjoy the stars. You can't see them back in Tucson like here."

"They do sparkle like diamonds on dark blue velvet out here in the desert."

She slid her fingers through his, enjoying this slice of intimacy with him after a busy day full of family and laughter, along with too much alcohol on her mom's part, damn it. She wished moments like these weren't so few and far between these days. A life with him in Tucson worried her. She could breathe out here in the wide open. The bustle of the city too often smothered her with doubts about her lack of a career, piling on the insecurities for added suffocation.

Wasn't there some way of meeting in the middle? Mac's job was important to him. She didn't want to pull him away from that after all the years of work he'd put into building his career.

"Claire," he said, stroking her hand with his thumb.

Was there a question in that or was he just saying her name? She stayed quiet, waiting to see.

"There's something I want to ask you." He stared out toward the dark desert, his body stiffening slightly.

"Okay," she said, encasing his hand with both of hers.

He took a deep breath before plunging onward. "Is being a low risk on paper a good or bad thing?"

"With Dad, it's a very good thing." She burrowed closer to him. "He likes you."

"Because I'm so steady and stable," he said more than asked, and didn't sound happy about it.

She frowned at him. "No, because you love me, and he can tell." She shifted on the step to give her tailbone a break. "There's nothing wrong with being steady and stable, Mac."

He grunted in disagreement.

"I think that's why I'm so gaga about you." She squeezed his hand between hers, trying to press her feelings into him.

"Claire, you don't have to—"

"I know I don't, but it's true. You know how crazy my family is. And in the midst of the chaos, here you are. Strong. Wonderfully grounded. Big hearted." She shoulder-bumped him. "Sexy as hell with your long legs and hazel eyes."

He glanced her way, his smile charming. "Don't forget that I'm an incredible stud between the sheets."

She giggled. "And that. Plus, you put up with my mother. That fact makes you extra golden in my book."

"Deborah is a force of nature, that's for sure. Sort of like a volcanic explosion followed by soul-scorching pyroclastic flows."

"If it's any consolation, I think she is more keen on you than Grady and his badge."

"That's not saying much." He sniffed. "How is your mom after your dad's visit?"

"She's still clutching that cognac bottle." Claire leaned her head against his shoulder. "I'm worried about her." She let out a harsh laugh. "How do you like that? After years of putting up with her picking at me ..."

"You're a good kid, Slugger." He kissed the top of her head. "You didn't deserve that candy coal in your stocking."

She smiled. "It was funny, though. Especially the fact that Kate got more coal than Ronnie and me. I guess Mom still has a sense of humor in spite of the mess with Dad."

The porch light turned on, followed by the screen door creaking open behind them.

"Claire," Gramps said. "You out here?"

"Yep."

"I have bad news."

Claire and Mac both turned toward him.

"What has Mom done now?" she asked, her gut tightening.

"Besides spill her drink on her fancy dress, nothing. It's Chester."

"What about him?"

"He fell through the back deck."

"Don't you mean fell off the deck?"

"No, he fell through it. Those dry-rotted boards finally gave way under his lard ass." Gramps snickered. "You're going to need to fix that."

"Fine. I'll patch it up tomorrow."

"I don't want a patch. I want a new back deck."

"What? That's going to take a lot of time and money."

"I've got the money and it's not like you're running off to join the Peace Corps any time soon."

Or ever. There were too many stinging and biting bugs involved in those Peace Corps jobs.

"Maybe call your cousin," he added. "See if she can spare a week or two to come down and help."

Claire's cousin Natalie lived up in Deadwood, South

Dakota. She took after Gramps when it came to carpentry and was far more talented with tools than Claire.

"It would be fun to have Natalie here for New Year's."

"Yep. She might like a vacation from the snow." The screen door creaked again. "I'll let you two lovebirds get back to your stargazing."

The porch light went out and then they were back to being alone under the stars.

A cold breeze rustled the strand of Christmas lights.

Claire shivered. "How do you feel about helping me and Natalie build a back deck?"

"You just want to watch my huge muscles as I lift heavy boards."

"Yeah, baby. You're one big stocking full of man candy."

"You will be wearing your tool belt, right?" He wiggled his eyebrows at her.

"Of course."

"Then I'll be there with bells on." He pushed to his feet, pulling her with him. "Come on. Let's go inside and rescue Grady from your mom."

"Ahh, but it's so fun to watch the sheriff squirm and writhe in agony under the heat."

He held the door for her. "You're just bitter about that jail cell of his."

"Damned straight." She paused in front of him, going up on her tiptoes under the mistletoe Chester had stapled to the top of the door frame to give him a kiss. "Merry Christmas, Mac," she whispered. "I have a naughty present for you later."

He brushed his lips over her forehead. "I was hoping you would, because I've been a very good boy this year."

"You sure have." She grabbed him by the sleeve, towing him through the General Store behind her.

"So, tell me more about this present."

She glanced back at him. "I learned a trick the other night

at Dirty Gerties that I want to show you when we're alone."

"A trick, you say?" He hit the brakes, tugging her to a stop. "Does it involve tassels or other fun accessories?"

She laughed, patting his chest. "No tassels, McGorgeous. But there are some jingle balls thrown in for additional merrymaking."

The End ... For Now

WAIT!

Later yet ...

"Kate, come to bed already," Butch hollered from their bedroom on the other side of the bathroom door.

"Just give me one more minute to get ready," she called back, safely tucking the Maya knife away in a small, velvet-lined case.

Finally tonight, for the first time since Kate had pocketed the knife at Dirty Gerties, she'd been able to sneak down into Ruby's office without anyone seeing her. She'd found the case right where her mom had said it was on their way home from Dirty Gerties. Claire and Ronnie had been pretty wasted at the strip club when Kate had pocketed it and they'd been asleep in the back seat when she'd grilled Deborah for more information about it.

Her mother didn't seem to remember the night's events, let alone the knife. Or she might think she'd lost it somewhere while drunk and was keeping quiet to save her hide. Either way, Kate was now the keeper of the knife, and she had plans to do some more digging and figure out where it had come from originally, be it a museum or private collection.

Surely someone must be missing it.

"Get ready for what?" Butch asked.

"I have a surprise going-away gift for you."

She opened the cupboard door in the sink vanity and stuffed the case in the back corner of the bottom shelf, behind an array of cleaning supplies. She was pretty sure it would be safe there until she had more time to look into its origins.

"Is the surprise something to do with why you snuck down to your grandfather's basement earlier?" Butch asked.

Son of a roasted chestnut! He'd seen her.

"I wasn't sneaking, dear. I was just checking to see that Mom put something back where she'd found it."

She looked in the mirror, hoping he didn't notice her cheeks were pinker than normal from the cloak-and-dagger excitement. She swished some minty mouthwash around in her mouth for a few seconds, and then spritzed her cleavage with his favorite perfume.

"Put what back?"

She hit the lights and opened the bathroom door, sauntering toward where he lay in bed under the covers with his arms crossed behind his head. "That's not important right now," she said in what she hoped was a throaty, sexy voice.

He frowned up at her. "Are you catching a cold?"

"No." She shrugged out of her silk robe and stood in front of him in the short satin, lace, and white fur see-through ensemble she'd bought as part of his Christmas gifts. "But I'm hoping to catch a man tonight."

He ogled high and low and then back up high, his gaze finally settling on hers. "You got a man in mind?"

"Well, there was this cute guy I saw at the gas station the

other day, but he didn't seem interested in blondes, so you'll have to suffice."

"Oh, I'll do more than just 'suffice,' Mrs. Claus." In a flash, he'd whipped back the covers, caught her around the waist, and pulled her down onto the warm bed beside him. "I'm going to shimmy down your chimney tonight."

She snorted. "Valentine, that's so bad."

He leaned down and kissed her, soft and slow, as his hands explored his Christmas present. What he was doing with his lips now, though, was good. Very good.

"Kate," he whispered as he kissed his way down her neck.

"What?"

He paused, looking up at her with one eyebrow quirked. "You didn't get into anything down in Ruby's office that is going to land you in trouble with Grady when I'm at my parents', did you?"

"Nah. Don't worry, baby."

His forehead lined. "Did your left eye just twitch?"

Rather than answer that, she reached down and pulled on the strings of the red satin bow above her cleavage, teasing him with a good dose of bared flesh. "Shush up and open your gift."

He groaned. With his ogle back in full force, he did just that—well, that and quite a lot more.

Later, as she lay with her head resting on his chest, watching the glittering lights on the small, lighted fake tree in the corner, she smiled. "Merry Christmas, Valentine."

He made a soft growly sound in his chest and trailed his fingers over her bare back. "Do you think you'll marry me and put me out of my misery before Santa comes back around next year?"

"Maybe." She shifted, crossing her arms over his sternum and resting her chin on them. "But first, we'll need to check if you were naughty or nice."

He tucked a strand of hair behind her ear. "You do know

that you're making me crazy, don't you?"

She closed her eyes, her heart full for the moment. "That makes two of us, Valentine."

Sliding down onto the bed beside him, she burrowed into his heat. As she began to drift off to sleep, the visions of bouncing jingle balls and dancing sugarplums gave way to thoughts about that Maya knife. Safely tucked away, it wouldn't be causing any trouble for her family. Not on Kate's watch anyway.

At least she hoped not.

The End ... For Now

Merry Christmas from the Morgan sisters and the rest of the Jackrabbit Junction crew!

Want to find out what happens next for the Morgan sisters? Grab your copy of Book 5 of the Jackrabbit Junction Mystery series, *IN CAHOOTS WITH THE PRICKLY PEAR POSSE*, and have a fun time spending New Year's Eve with Claire, Kate, Ronnie, Mac, and their cousin, Natalie (who co-stars in the Deadwood Mystery Series with Violet Parker). Bring in the New Year with plenty of giggles, snorts, laughs, and a bit of suspense!

Ann Charles is a USA Today bestselling author who writes award-winning mysteries that are splashed with humor, romance, paranormal, and whatever else she feels like throwing into the mix. When she is not dabbling in fiction, arm-wrestling with her children, attempting to seduce her husband, or arguing with her sassy cats, she is daydreaming of lounging poolside at a fancy resort with a blended margarita in one hand and a great book in the other.

Facebook (Personal Page):
http://www.facebook.com/ann.charles.author

Facebook (Author Page):
http://www.facebook.com/pages/Ann-Charles/37302789804?ref=share

Instagram:
https://www.instagram.com/ann_charles

YouTube Channel:
https://www.youtube.com/user/AnnCharlesAuthor

Twitter (as Ann W. Charles):
http://twitter.com/AnnWCharles

Ann Charles Website:
http://www.anncharles.com

More Books by Ann

www.anncharles.com

The Jackrabbit Junction Mystery Series

Bestseller in Women Sleuth Mystery and Romantic Suspense

Welcome to the Dancing Winnebagos RV Park. Down here in Jackrabbit Junction, Arizona, Claire Morgan and her rabble-rousing sisters are really good at getting into trouble—BIG trouble (the land your butt in jail kind of trouble). This rowdy, laugh out loud mystery series is packed with action, suspense, adventure, and relationship snafus. Full of colorful characters and twisted-up plots, the stories of the Morgan sisters will keep you wondering what kind of a screwball mess they are going to land in next.

The Deadwood Mystery Series

WINNER of the 2010 Daphne du Maurier Award for Excellence in Mystery/Suspense

WINNER of the 2011 Romance Writers of America® Golden Heart Award for Best Novel with Strong Romantic Elements

Welcome to Deadwood—the Ann Charles version. The world I have created is a blend of present day and past, of fiction and non-fiction. What's real and what isn't is for you to determine as the series develops, the characters evolve, and I write the stories line by line. I will tell you one thing about the series—it's going to run on for quite a while, and Violet Parker will have to hang on and persevere through the crazy adventures I have planned for her. Poor, poor Violet. It's a good thing she has a lot of gumption to keep her going!

The Deadwood Shorts Series

The Deadwood Shorts collection includes short stories featuring the characters of the Deadwood Mystery series. Each tale not only explains more of Violet's history, but also gives a little history of the other characters you know and love from the series. Rather than filling the main novels in the series with these short side stories, I've put them into a growing Deadwood Shorts collection for more reading fun.

The Deadwood Undertaker Series

From the bestselling, multiple award-winning, humorous Deadwood Mystery series comes a new herd of tales set in the same Deadwood stomping grounds, only back in the days when the Old West town was young.

The Dig Site Mystery Series

Welcome to the jungle—the steamy Maya jungle that is, filled with ancient ruins, deadly secrets, and quirky characters. Quint Parker, renowned photojournalist (and lousy amateur detective), is in for a whirlwind of adventure and suspense as he and archaeologist Dr. Angélica García get tangled up in mysteries from the past and present in exotic dig sites. Loaded with action and laughs, along with all sorts of steamy heat, these books will keep you sweating along with the characters as they do their best to make it out of the jungle alive.

The AC Silly Circus Series

From AC Silly Circus Co. comes a series of paranormal mystery novellas chock-full of oddball shapeshifters, dangerous secrets, spicy steam, and loads of laughs.

Made in the USA
Middletown, DE
29 April 2023

29705403R00076